MORE CLUES TO THE EXCITEMENT ABOUT

R O B E R T   B A R N A R D

SCHOOL
FOR
MURDER

Robert Barnard

A DELL BOOK

Published by
Dell Publishing Co., Inc.
1 Dag Hammarskjold Plaza
New York, New York 10017

Published in Britain as *Little Victims*

Dell ® TM 681510, Dell Publishing Co., Inc.

ISBN: 0-440-17605-0

Reprinted by arrangement with Charles Scribner's Sons

Printed in the United States of America
First Dell printing—March 1985

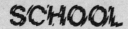

SCHOOL

FOR

MURDER

CHAPTER 1

STAFF MEETING

A fly buzzed in the Staff Common Room of Burleigh School. It provided a fitting accompaniment to the voice of the headmaster.

'I sometimes think that the Oxford and Cambridge Examination Board has taken leave of its senses,' said Mr Crumwallis, in his inconsequential tenor drone. 'First it was someone called Golding, then it was Weskit or some such name, and now it's a woman with a name like a Victorian tart, who writes books about girls who get pregnant by homosexuals. Is this the kind of stuff for teenage boys? What was wrong with *Black Arrow*, I'd like to know? Or *Westward Ho?*'

Or, to put the matter more honestly, thought Dorothea Gilberd, tearing her glance from Tom Tedder, why don't they prescribe books that Burleigh School has already got copies of? Miss Gilberd (Junior English, Junior History and Junior anything going) had had, over the years, more than her fill of *Black Arrow*.

'I'm sure I will have the support of Mr McWhirter in any representations I may feel called upon to make to the Board,' said the headmaster.

Iain Ogilvy McWhirter (Senior English and Religious Instruction) had been asleep for the past ten minutes, but Tom Tedder (Art and Woodwork) said 'Arrgh' through closed lips, and that seemed to do well enough.

The bust of Gibbon, purchased in Geneva during the headmaster's first post-war vacation, sneered down on him as he proceeded.

'Then there is the question of . . . metalwork.' The

headmaster wielded that pause with all the virtuosity of Edith Evans in her prime. Nobody could doubt that metalwork was going to get its comeuppance. Nobody, indeed, who knew anything of the school's finances, could have doubted that its prospects were nil. 'It has been suggested to me by the parents of Tomkiss and Wattling that their sons are skilled in . . . metalwork, and that the school should have an . . . option that would enable them to pursue their interest in this . . . field. Other schools, they inform me, *offer* . . . metalwork. But then, other schools, I am informed, *offer* their young gentlemen courses in car maintenance. Or bricklaying. And in any case the question of *should* we, may be pre-empted by the question of *can* we offer such a course . . .'

You mean old sod, thought Tom Tedder, torn between a consciousness of Dorothea Gilberd's eyes on him again and some residual interest in the subject in hand. You wouldn't offer them art if you didn't see the chance of slapping on the cost of paint as an extra. If you could just pick up a load of scrap iron and shove it on the bill under metalwork you wouldn't be turning up your nose at the subject. If I had any guts I'd walk out of the front door now, this minute, and I'd hitch my way to Italy and rent a shack in Tuscany, and I'd paint trash to sell to the tourists in the Piazza della Signoria, and I'd paint . . .

But what else he could paint, other than trash for the tourists, brought him back to earth.

'. . . but even were we able to come to some agreement with the authorities at Cullbridge Comprehensive, they would demand, would they not, a *quid pro quo?* And what are we in a position to offer them? I hardly think they would be interested in using our gymnasium. Even on his last visit, two years ago, the Ministry Inspector declared that it would soon be more of a hazard to health than a promoter of it.'

Taking advantage of this unusual spurt of self-criticism, Bill Muggeridge (P. E., Games and Religious Instruction) threw forward a hefty fist and said: 'In that connection, Headmaster—'

'But then what do these Ministry Inspectors know about education?' resumed the headmaster hastily, discarding doubts as quickly as he had assumed them. 'About schools, no doubt, they know something—perhaps they have schedules and inventories that tell them in wearisome detail what they should look for in the *structure*, the physical fabric. But to the soul of a school, to education itself, they are blind. I question, personally, whether these inspectors have not outlived their usefulness. It is not as though the country were riddled with Dotheboys Halls!'

A snuffle of laughter from the body of the meeting was hastily suppressed. Please God, thought Penny Warlock (Junior Classics, Geography and Religious Instruction), get me a job in a real school before next September. Please God let me be doing real work. Penny Warlock, twenty-three, pretty and serious-minded, believed in God, and her words were not random aspirations. But they lacked conviction, because she could not believe in a God who answered prayers. If God answered prayers, why was she here? Why were any of them here?

'So if Tomkiss and Wattling feel impelled to express their artistic bent in any form of . . . metalwork, it will have to be, I fear, in their own time, and at their parents' expense. And so we come to the antepenultimate item on the agenda. The vacant position of matron.'

'If I might say a few words, Headmaster, on that,' put in Glenda Grower (History, French and World Religions if absolutely pressed). Her voice, like everything about her, rang confidently, but the headmaster was not to be put off his stride.

'Really, Miss Grower, this *is* a staff meeting. As I was saying, the position of matron has now been vacant since term began, and in spite of valiant efforts to fill the position — '

'Too mean to offer a living wage,' muttered Tom Tedder to the young man beside him.

'— we have been unable to fill the position. Meanwhile, as you know, my good wife has stepped in to fill the breach, and — '

Goaded beyond endurance by the reference to the headmaster's wife, to whom she had that morning sent a boy with a high fever, only to have him sent back with iodine on his knuckles, Glenda Grower chimed in again in her rich, ringing voice:

'I would remind you, Headmaster, that small as our boarding section is, the Ministry recommendation is that for any establishment of twenty boarders or more, a qualified matron be employed. Grateful as we are, of course, to Mrs Crumwallis for her sterling . . . efforts.'

The headmaster regarded her with disfavour.

'As I was about to say, this situation cannot be allowed to continue, trespassing as we are on my wife's time and goodwill. Efforts will therefore continue to find a suitable person before the commencement of next term. My penultimate item is that term ends on April 13th, and reports and class lists should be in my office one week before then. And the final item: I move that we all adjourn to my sitting-room for a glass of sherry."

Penny Warlock perked up. This was the first sensible suggestion she had heard from the headmaster since she had come to Burleigh School, one week after the beginning of Spring term (her predecessor having expired, Kennedy's Latin Primer in hand, in the middle of the pluperfect of *Amo* with Form 2B). She let Glenda Grower lead the way, splendidly striding forward with that swing that showed off her tall, slim figure, and watched the other, older members of staff follow in her wake. Together with Toby Freely, the fresh-faced young man who had been sitting next to Tom Tedder, she brought up, modestly, the rear of the exodus.

'Best thing that's happened since I arrived,' she muttered to him, as they shuffled along the lino'd passage towards the headmaster's quarters.

'Absolutely,' said Toby. 'I suppose I'll get some, will I? They couldn't not.'

'You poor young things,' said Corbett Farraday (Physics, Chemistry, and anything vaguely in that line) who was flapping his overgrown boy scout's body along with the mass of teachers, and now looked around at them with his unnaturally innocent expression. 'What a jolly lot you have to learn.'

And certainly the atmosphere was less than festive in the headmaster's sitting-room. Near the fireplace a table had been installed, and on it placed two bottles. Behind the bottles stood Mrs Crumwallis — tall, bony, straggly of hair, the only memorable feature about her being her large, round, immensely thick-lensed glasses. As each slightly shamefaced figure came up to the table, she peered intently at the face, muttered 'Sweet or dry?' and then poured from one of her bottles as if administering Syrup of Figs or Cod Liver Oil to the infant sick.

The older men established themselves over by the fireplace. The central position was taken by the headmaster himself, and the live coals sent vivid warmth to his posterior. Edward Crumwallis was tall, sunken-cheeked, and he bent his neck and head forward towards his companions, making him look like a bird of prey with indigestion. Next to him on his left, keeping as far as possible from the coals as though to emphasize his lack of pretensions to warmth, was Percy Makepeace ('We're distantly welated to the Thackeways'), the pale shred of a mathematics teacher. On the headmaster's right, encroaching rather than retreating, was Septimus Coffin, sixty-odd if he was a day, retired grammar school classics teacher. A bachelor with a sister as housekeeper, he had found retirement unstimulating, and had been pleased to come back to teaching at any price, any place. He was swilling his sherry with a will, and tugging at his bushy, nicotine-stained moustache as if he expected it to come off.

'Evenings are drawing out,' said the headmaster.

'Yes, indeed,' said Mr Makepeace.

It was Septimus Coffin's weakness that, after a lifetime of schoolmastering, he could never leave alone the flat, meaningless cliché.

'Yes, indeed,' he said. 'Surprising if they weren't, what? If it were March and we were still drawing the curtains at four. Frightening to contemplate, what? Earth stopped on its axle, or whatever you call it.'

'So heartening,' said Mr Makepeace, terrified to the depths of his timid soul by Coffin's tendency to seize on the headmaster's least utterances, brandish them around, then publicly trample on them. 'So heartening, the coming of Spring. The new green—'

'Green, eh?' said Septimus. 'Whatever next?'

'—the buds coming out, the crocuses coming up.'

'The fuel bills coming down,' said the headmaster.

At staff functions at Burleigh, little groups tended to form. For example, by the drinks table Bill Muggeridge seemed to be trying to make up to Mrs Crumwallis. They made an odd pair, she bony and remote, he heavy, grubby and vaguely disreputable. What they could have in common it would be difficult to guess, unless it was that both were defiantly unacademic and felt the need to make a common front against the teachers—not that learning sat particularly heavy on any of them, either. At any rate, if an alliance was being formed, it was as heavy going as bringing together two Middle East states. Mrs Crumwallis was peering at Bill Muggeridge as if he were some little-known species of the rhinoceros family, and she needed to consult the label on his cage to be sure of his name.

On occasions such as this, Dorothea Gilberd tended to gravitate towards Tom Tedder. On occasions such as this, and also on occasions such as coffee breaks, exam supervision and staff booze-ups. She flattered herself this was done discreetly, and was noticed by no one, though the yearning in her look as she gazed at him would be obvious to a child of five, and the staff made frequent jokes about her loving him with a love that made his life a burden. This was not, in fact, true. Tom Tedder — bulky, untidy, and God-dammit-I'm-an-artist in his approach to the world in general — accepted the situation quite calmly, as most men of forty will accept devotion, even from a woman a dozen years his senior.

'I must say,' said Miss Gilberd, 'that however much that precious trio over there may burble on, I don't see much sign of Spring.'

'I never really notice things like that during term time,' said Tom Tedder. 'I think I go into a sort of visual hibernation. Of course, when it's vacation, and I can paint more . . .'

'I don't think the seasons *mean* much anymore, though,' continued Miss Gilberd eagerly, 'not in an English town, anyway. Now, if this were Italy . . .'

She had touched the right spring. She always did. She had made great capital out of a fortnight's bus tour to Lake Garda.

'Ah!' said Tom Tedder.

'Spring on the Adriatic coast!'

'Winter in the Dolomites!'

' "Thick as autumnal leaves that strow the brooks in Vallombrosa," ' quoted Dorothea Gilberd, going slightly pink.

'I saw Siena for the first time in Autumn,' said Tom

Tedder, with a catch in his voice.

'Wonderful Siena. The cathedral must be a dream for an artist.'

Tom Tedder reined in his emotion.

'When I painted it, it looked like a bloody great liquorice allsort,' he said. Tom Tedder's tragedy was that he had a perfectly accurate estimate of his own talents as an artist.

Over by the fireplace, the headmaster had exhausted his limited store of small talk and had advanced to matters of serious educational concern.

'As far as I can see,' he said, blinking magisterially, 'this decision by the European Court is going to have far-reaching consequences. Ver-ry far-reach-ing.'

'Weally, Headmaster?' said Mr Makepeace.

'It spells the beginning of the end of corporal punishment in British schools.'

'Heavens above!' said Septimus Coffin. 'How are the Scottish schools going to manage?'

'How, indeed?' said the headmaster, who was tormented with indecision whenever he spoke with Septimus Coffin, how far to take him seriously. 'It's another victory for the "reformers", I'm afraid. One explains to them over and over again the benefits: it's quick, cheap, no hard feelings on either side—'

'Considerable enjoyment on one,' said Coffin.

'Quite . . . quite. But they won't listen. They charge ahead with their ill-advised new brooms. The Burleigh School has never, I hope, had the reputation of a beating school, but this will inevitably change the character of the place.'

'I hope that point was put to the powers-that-be in Strasbourg,' said Septimus Coffin. 'Too busy fattening their geese to listen, I suppose. Well, well—to think the days of bottom-slippering are numbered. I think I need another sherry to face up to that prospect.'

*

The rest of the teachers, or most of them, stood awkwardly together in the middle of the room. Glenda Grower stood a little aside, as she so often did — splendid, cool, apart. Penny Warlock, Toby Freely and Corbett Farraday grouped themselves around a rickety occasional table, on which was perched one of Mrs Crumwallis's repulsive collections of cacti. This one was thick and protruberant, and bent unexpectedly at the top: it looked like a cross between a penis and a corkscrew, and the little group looked at it as if wondering who would dare be first to point this out.

'What's happened to old McWhirter?' said Penny, deciding not to mention the comparison in the company of two young men who gave her some gratifying doggy devotion.

'He nipped off,' said Toby Freely. 'Well, hardly nipped. I saw him doing a side shuffle to the main entrance as we all trooped along here. Presumably he's not to be soft-soaped by a glass of Amontillado.'

'Black mark against *his* name,' said Penny.

'*What* greenhorns you are,' said Glenda Grower, shaking her great mass of long, auburn hair from over her eyes. 'You don't understand the situation here at all, do they, Corbett? Mr McWhirter does what he likes at Burleigh, and the reason is that Mr McWhirter has money in the place.'

'Money?' said Toby, incredulous.

'Yes, indeed,' said Corbett Farraday, in his enthusiastic, puppyish way. He was all of twenty-nine, but he acted thirteen, and he had great rolls of fat on his tummy, the result of unwise motherly feeding. He rested his glass on the paunch now, regarded them owlishly, and gave the impression, as always, of someone who had not gone through the usual process of growing up, but had remained a toddler, magnified to the nth degree. 'Isn't it incredible? I mean, would you jolly well put money into this place? But I had it from Makepeace, who was here at the time. Three years ago, it was, and the school was nearly on the rocks. You can imagine: old Crumwallis going around with the expression of a Soviet agronomist at harvest time. Then along comes old McWhirter and says he will plonk his life savings in the school.'

'I knew he was mad.'

'Six months later, comprehensive education comes in in the county of Swessex. Burleigh School starts looking up.'

'You could have fooled me,' said Penny Warlock bitterly.

'Comparatively,' said Glenda Grower. 'At least the bills get paid. We get paid — very little, I hear you cry, but we get paid, and on the right day of the month. I will refrain from horror stories of Burleigh's past, but I assure you, Corbett is right. Things have looked up.'

' "Glory and honour unto him, be unto him," ' said Corbett Farraday. 'McWhirter, saviour of the day and hero of the hour.'

'I say,' said Penny, losing interest in the fortunes of Burleigh School, which she hoped speedily to put behind her, 'look at that. Old Coffin is going back to the sherry table. I think he's going to ask for more. Too *Oliver Twist* for words. Do you think he'll get it? He is — he's getting it. My God, I'm going to try that.'

Glenda Grower gave Corbett Farraday the look old pros give when confronted by the naïvetés of fresh-faced amateurs.

As Penny went over to the drinks table the headmaster was in full spate. Though he had no great stock of small talk he had a great store of commonplaces, which could be adapted to any subject.

'There it is, I'm afraid,' he was saying, 'that's the way it is today. When Europe speaks we click our heels and fall into line. Wasn't like that in 'forty-five, eh, Coffin?'

'Nor in 'eighteen,' said Coffin. 'Eh, Crumwallis?'

'What it means,' pursued the headmaster, ignoring him, 'is first a gentle directive from the Ministry, then sterner ones, and so on.'

'But surely the Ministwy can't touch us, Headmaster?' said Percy Makepeace, uneasy at the thought of still more horrendous disorder in his classes.

'They can make life damned unpleasant for us if we don't toe the line,' said Edward Crumwallis. 'No, I can see what this means: it's the end of beating in our time.'

Penny Warlock, cringing under the intense peer of Mrs Crumwallis, pricked up her ears. She wasn't a fanatic, but she did think the slipper was used a bit too freely on the younger boys.

'Is that a directive, Headmaster?' she said.

Edward Crumwallis did one of his characteristic swerves, and went abruptly off in the other direction.

'A directive? Oh dear me, no, young lady. Why anticipate the evil hour? These jumped up jacks-in-office have things all too much their own way. No doubt we can drag our heels pretty effectively if we really try. Go by stages. Perhaps we could first take the right to slipper away from the prefects.'

'They won't like that,' said Septimus Coffin. 'One of the perks of office. Pretty much the only damned perk they have.'

'Perhaps we can bring it in next year,' said the head. 'When Hilary Frome is head boy. Frome could certainly bring it off without any trouble.'

It was odd. At the mention of Hilary Frome a sudden silence fell over the room. The other teachers had been drifting towards the fire, anticipating, perhaps, a bit of an argy about beating, or a discussion of the pros and cons of Europe. But now they stopped, shifted in embarrassment, and Tom Tedder cast a sidelong glance at Miss

Gilberd, and raised his eyebrows. Bill Muggeridge opened his mouth to say something, but happily only bad breath came out. The headmaster noticed nothing. He expected silence when he spoke, almost required it, and the more worshipful the better.

'Ah yes, Frome can bring it in. A boy with a great deal of tact and delicacy.'

'A refined thug,' muttered Tom Tedder to Dorothea Gilberd.

'I congratulate myself, in fact, on the idea of nominating him as head boy designate,' pursued Edward Crumwallis. 'Quite an inspiration. It takes the burden off Widgery in the lead-up to the GCE, and it gives Frome himself invaluable experience.'

'It was the only way he could be sure of keeping him here next year,' muttered Glenda Grower to Penny Warlock.

'I observed him myself only last week, at the planning session for the all-Swessex schools athletics meeting. He has manner, that boy. Presence. He makes himself felt.'

A monster, thought Percy Makepeace, tears squeezing themselves into his eyes. A trouble-maker, a stirrer-up, a tormentor.

'No doubt the rest of you will be able to see him in action next week, on Parents' Evening,' proceeded Mr Crumwallis, smoothly bland.

'Parents' Evening?' said Penny Warlock.

'Parents' Evening,' repeated the head irritably. 'Parents' Evening is *always* the third Thursday in March.'

'This is my first term here,' said Penny defensively.

'Well, you really must try to familiarize yourself with our traditions. What was I saying when I was interrupted? Ah yes. Frome has already expressed his willingness to help Mrs Crumwallis with the refreshments. He will organize the more presentable of the boarders to do the serving. I have no doubt he will make an excellent impression on the parents. A good-looking boy. Quiet in his manner, but very confident.'

His assembled staff stared stonily back, as he looked round at them, apparently calling for some kind of congratulations. But the head seemed unable to leave the subject. As if seized with prophetic fire he raised his eyes to the ceiling, and said:

'I predict that Frome is really going to make The Burleigh School talked about!'

There was no visible reaction to this prophetic vision. No one suggested weaving a circle round the headmaster thrice, in view of the fact that he had obviously fed on honeydew and drunk the milk of paradise. All there was was an awkward clearing of throats and a gazing at shoes. Then Glenda Grower, the most strong-minded of the staff, put her glass down on the table and made obvious going-away gestures. Penny Warlock decided to follow suit.

It was at this point that Mrs Crumwallis spoke aloud for the first time.

'Miss Grower? That will be 40p. Miss Warlock? *Two* glasses, Miss Warlock—that'll be 80p. Forty, Mr Freely, and one pound twenty, Mr Muggeridge. No, it can't wait till tomorrow.'

'You poor children,' said Glenda Grower, turning to Penny Warlock and Toby as they slunk away. 'You've so much to learn. This is how all social occasions at Burleigh end.'

CHAPTER 2

BURLEIGH

The position of Burleigh School in the English educational system would be very difficult to explain to a foreigner (who has, God knows, enough to contend with in comprehending the other parts of the system). Nor would it be possible to refer him to any works of literature (before the present one) from which he could gain enlightenment. The prep schools have had their Orwell, the public schools their Connolly and Benedictus, the convent schools their Antonia White, the private boarding-schools their Waugh and Nicholas Blake. No one has thought it worth their while to eulogize or anathematize schools like Burleigh. Indeed, schools like Burleigh do not seem to be the sort of places from which writers emerge.

And yet, any medium-sized town in the southern half of England has its Burleigh School: a private day school to which, for a not too exorbitant fee, parents can send their children and boast that they are privately educated. Not well educated, but privately. Burleigh itself had been founded — no, started — between the wars, had survived the Depression (as the South of England middle classes in general had so signally managed to coast blithely through the Depression) and had offered over the years an alternative to the Grammar, Secondary Modern and Technical Schools of the town of Cullbridge. Which meant, in effect, that though some parents chose to send their children there rather than to the Grammar School, many more sent them there because they failed their eleven-plus, that Beecher's Brook of English childhood. With the coming of comprehensive education three years before, even the faint whiff of privilege attached to the Grammar School had evaporated, a fact on which Burleigh had been able to capitalize, in a mild way.

Foreigners are always apt to find charming the examples they come across of quaint anachronisms, of dated anomalies, in English life. One such charming and dated anomaly is that a school like Burleigh can be bought. A man — any man — can buy such a place, set himself up as headmaster, and run it as he likes. Indeed, that is precisely what Edward Crumwallis had done. He had bought it from its previous aging owner/headmaster in 1969, and had been there ever since. This must not be taken to imply that Edward Crumwallis was unfit for his position. He was in fact a BA (3rd class, Geography) from the University of Hull (graduated 1948). Still, scholarship was not exactly his thing. He might take the odd class in Geography at a pinch, but he had never given the subject any particular prominence in the school, and most boys gave it up after two years. Nor was Crumwallis anxious to take over periods in other subjects when there was need — as in cases of sickness or (frequently) death. Since his graduation he had not cultivated Learning. He had cultivated Manner. He had bought Burleigh (which he invariably called The Burleigh School, in capitals) precisely so that his manner might be given free rein and ample pasturage. A very good manner it was too, with parents — decidedly impressive. It certainly impressed those of limited intelligence, among whom may be numbered Crumwallis himself. He really believed in it: he not only thought that others should remain silent during his threadbare pontifications, but he actually believed they would benefit from them. Such a conspicuous lack of self-knowledge has its dangers.

Not that the Manner — which he intended should be so admired later in the week on Parents' Evening — was particularly in evidence on the Monday, as he sat at his study desk and went over the plans for that event with his wife. The side of Edward Crumwallis that was most evident during such tête-à-têtes was the petty-minded, niggling side (that side of his psychological profile that was seldom turned in the parents' direction).

'The question is, shall we splurge on the coffee and scrimp on the tea, or vice versa,' he was saying, in that thin, scratchy voice of his that his wife did not seem to notice. 'Now, which parents who matter are coming, and what do they generally drink?'

Enid Crumwallis, behind her pebble glasses, might be seen to screw up her eyes. This was the sort of question that her intellect most enjoyed exercising itself on. She had a mind like a computer, with indefinite retrieval of unimportant facts.

'Well, now—Mr and Mrs Quigly are coming, and they drink tea. And so do Mrs Patterson and the Reverend Martins. On the other hand Major Tilney usually drinks coffee . . .'

'Ah—pity.'

'But then, Dr and Mrs Frome almost always take tea.'

'That settles it. Tea it is. I'll say to the Major 'I particularly recommend the tea.' Get a good, straight-forward Ceylon. Earl Grey never goes down well in a boys' school—there's that touch of Milady's Boudoir about it. And instant coffee. Now, biscuits—shall we say two per parent? Yes, two.'

'Marie biscuits,' catalogued his wife.

'And some sort of non-alcoholic fruit cup for the boarders who do the serving out.'

'Is that necessary?' asked his wife, who had all the instincts that would, a century ago, have made her a successful workhouse mistress.

'I'm afraid so. The parents are quick to seize on anything that might suggest we use boys as unpaid labour. A sad reflection on human nature, and the times we live in, but true. Some sort of squash will do, but put some slices of apple and orange in, to make it look something special.'

The festive deliberations were interrupted by a knock at the door.

'Oh, Mr Crumwallis, I'm awfully sorry to interrupt—'

Miss Dorothea Gilberd's comfortable face came round the door, and then her comfortable figure came in.

'Awfully sorry. I can see you're busy. But Mother was *rather* poorly this morning, and I wondered if I might skip 2B English and just *rush* home and see to her a bit.'

Miss Gilberd was a great asset to Burleigh. Motherly but firm, ignorant but insistent on communicating what she did know, she was an excellent teacher for the lower forms. She knew her limitations better than she knew her worth, and she taught in a private school because it gave her a little more latitude to come and go as she wished— an important point, since she cared for an old mother whom eighty years had made exacting. Mr Crumwallis was very understanding. He wanted to keep her.

'I'm sure that can be arranged, Miss Gilberd. I expect Mr Freely will be willing to oblige.'

'It's only poetry . . .'

'Well, there should be no problem, then.'

'I'll be back after lunch.'

'Of course, of course. I know I can trust you . . . Oh, and Miss Gilberd—'

'Yes?'

'Those biscuits of yours that went down so *very* well at the last Parents' Evening. I wonder—'

Compliments always caught Miss Gilberd on the hop, she was so little used to them. She blushed.

'Of course, Headmaster. Only too happy . . .'

'Ah,' said Edward Crumwallis as she withdrew. 'A happy thought. Cross off the Maries.'

His wife stared, her piggy eyes speculative, at the door.

'You do realize, don't you, that she's in love with that Tom Tedder?'

Her husband laughed, a high sound like radiophonic interference on a shortwave band.

'Of course. We've discussed it many times, Enid. All to the good, you know. It might keep her here after that mother of hers dies.'

'What we discussed was infatuation,' said Enid Crumwallis, who had a fund of malapropisms acquired unconsciously from her cook. 'So far she's just been infaturated with him. But I was standing near her at prayers this morning. I saw her looking at him. It's gone beyond that now. It's love, that's what it is. Love.'

Edward Crumwallis let out more silvery squeaks of amusement.

'Good heavens, Enid, what nonsense. Love, infatuation: what would you know about that?'

What, indeed?

Dorothea Gilberd had already asked Toby Freely to take over her class in English. Toby was in fact if not in name in charge of the twenty-seven boarders at Burleigh, and he spent much of the day with nothing to do. In the afternoons he sometimes helped with games, or stood in for Bill Muggeridge in the gym, if Bill wanted to go home and check up on his wife (which he quite often did). Or he stood in for one or other of the teachers, notably Miss Gilberd when she wanted to 'pop home', or Mr McWhirter when he failed altogether to arrive. But quite a lot of the day Toby spent wandering around the school, not because he was naturally idle, but because it was his first job, and the school fascinated him. Sometimes he wondered how the teachers could go on living, knowing this was to be their life, until the end.

He would stand in the corridor which ran along past the junior classrooms, as he had done that morning, and listen to the lessons being given. Some of them, in fact, were perfectly good. Septimus Coffin could call on forty years of experience, and in so far as Latin could be made entertaining, he made it so. Glenda Grower was positively a genius. He could stand listening to her classes for hours. She stood there, tall, slim, striking, her hair catching light from the sun, and she told them about history or exotic religions—dramatically, humanly, but cleverly mixing in the dry bits with the drama.

But to stand outside listening to Percy Makepeace's classes, as he had done today, was to die a little. What went on there was not education, nor even the appearance of education. It was a good old traditional teacher-roasting.

'The square on the hypotenuse,' said Percy Makepeace for the tenth time.

'The square on the hippopotamus,' chorused three or four boys.

'Please sir, how did the hippopotamus get a square on him?' shrilled one teenage wit.

'It was a square hippopotamus to start with, you oaf,' yelled another.

'Please sir, is this Euclid?' came from the back of the room. It was a signal for one of their favourite litanies.

'You-clid!' came from one boy at the front.

'You-thanasia!' contributed a boy near the back.

'You-genics!'

'You-topia!'

'You-tube!'

If he lingered at the end of the corridor he could see the class without Percy Makepeace seeing him. But he knew what he would see. Seated in the middle of the uproar would be Hilary Frome, who was destined, according to the headmaster, to make Burleigh School talked about. At first sight one might think he was taking no part in the uproar, but Toby had only recently completed his own schooldays, and he had soon realized that Hilary controlled it. Percy Makepeace, too, knew that, and seldom took his eyes off him. He was a willowy boy, firm of body; his hair was fair, and a lock fell over his right eye. His lips were curled in contemptuous amusement — lips with a suggestion of fullness about them. He looked, Toby thought, the kind of boy who might play the passive role in some bent porno film — and, indeed, were he asked Hilary Frome would certainly have been willing. Hilary was a boy who saw himself as a connoisseur of experience.

It was not only Percy Makepeace who kept his eyes on Hilary. The boys contributing to the uproar did so as well, and were rewarded for any unusually telling stroke of humour (within the tradition-bound schoolboy framework) by a smirk of appreciation. He was conducting the whole thing, with a minimum of gesture: a sort of schoolboy Adrian Boult.

'Stop this noise! STOP THIS NOISE! If there is any more of this I shall weport you to the headmaster.'

'MAKE PEACE NOT WAR!' chorused the boys.

'You should love your neighbour, sir. Isn't that what you learn in church?' (Mr Makepeace's obsessive frequenting of High Anglican church services was well known.)

'Do you love your neighbour, sir? Is Willis your neighbour? Miss Warlock says everyone is your neighbour. Do you love Willis, sir?'

'Oh, *sir*,' said Willis, with elephantine coyness.

'I say,' said Hilary Frome, as the shrieks of laughter reached a crescendo. 'Isn't it about time we got down to some work? After all, you are paid to teach . . . sir.'

The class took it as a signal. Within thirty seconds they were all sitting, if not working, with some semblance of order. Out in the corridor Toby found he was sweating. He let out a long-held breath. How, he asked himself, how could one put up with that, day after day. He looked at his watch. Ten-forty. He would wait and see if Mr

McWhirter arrived, or if he would have to fill in. Because Mr McWhirter—he who had put money into the school—was in a privileged position, and he took every advantage of it.

But when he strolled out into the front drive, Mr McWhirter was being decanted from a neighbour's car at the front gate. Mr McWhirter had had his first two periods free, as usual, the timetable being constructed around Mr McWhirter's convenience and preferences. From the front gate he shuffled down the drive, a slow shuffle, because he was afflicted with chilblains. At periods of especial affliction he wore shoes slit down the side and stuffed with newspapers. He suffered a desperate need of heat, and on occasion would come to school with a great hole in the back calf of his trousers, surrounded by scorch marks. Next day he would come with a rough square tacked on to the inside. Before long, that too would be scorched. He looked, in fact, less like a man of academic attainment than a scarecrow kept in the garden of a man of academic attainment. Perhaps for this reason it was rumoured among the boys that he was a million-aire. He shuffled straight past Toby, eyes fixed straight ahead, and arrived at 4A one minute before his class was due to begin.

Toby, leaving a judicious interval, strolled back towards the classrooms. If Mr Makepeace was a study in how much inhumanity a man could bear, Mr McWhirter was a study in how non-human a man could become.

'*Macbeth*, Act One, Scene Seven,' he announced as the boys clattered in. His voice was harsh and nasal, as if it had had to fight a stiff battle around the bridge of his nose before it had been able to emerge at all.

' "If it were done when 'tis done, then 'twere well it were done quickly." The word "done" in its first appearance may be taken to mean "finished". "If the assassination / Could trammel up the consequence . . ." The word "trammel" here means . . .'

Iain Ogilvie McWhirter's teaching methods, Toby felt, were more than a little old-fashioned. In fact, it seemed that Burleigh School as a whole was untouched by modern educational theories. In this respect the boys were lucky. But Toby wondered whether the old-fashioned theories it conducted itself by were of the best, or consistently applied. He wondered, indeed, if some of the teachers were interested in anything other than getting through to three-thirty, filling up the time with something or other. Mr McWhirter's methods meant that some— any— excuse had to be found to interrupt his recital every ten minutes or so.

'Sir, sir,' said a boy. 'Sir, do you think *Macbeth* is a good play?'

It was a question calculated to arouse Mr McWhirter's scorn. He piped through his nasal tubes a snuffling laugh.

"If *you* think it a good play, all the better for you. And if you don't— you still have to do it.'

'Well, because, I mean, sir— we did it in 2A, and now we're doing it again, sir—'

'And we're doing it again next year for GCE,' drawled a voice that Toby recognized as Hilary Frome's.

'Oh no!' sighed the chorus.

'Well, you won't be able to say you don't know the play,' returned Iain McWhirter, with another nasal chortle.

'Actually,' said Hilary Frome, 'the school has only got *Macbeth*, *The Merchant of Venice*, and *Henry IV*, *Part I*, and *that's* why we have to do them so often. Look—' he held aloft his battered, ink-bespattered copy—'this one looks as if it's been in use since the Boer War.'

The trouble with Hilary Frome, thought Toby, was that he was so often right. Watching that fair, contemptuous face he thought how well he knew the type from his own school. But Hilary did not impress Mr McWhirter.

' "And catch with his surcease success," ' he intoned, and the class settled down to another ten minutes of drudgery.

It was at this point that Dorothea Gilberd, wandering round the school in search of him, came upon Toby. With a schoolboy's shamefacedness, as if he had been caught out in something furtive (as, really, he had), he agreed at once to take her class.

When he came to look at the poem Miss Gilberd had intended to teach, Toby rather wondered at her judgment. When he took classes for McWhirter he stuck to the Romantics, or things that one could get a good adolescent wallow out of: Housman, say, or *The Ballad of Reading Gaol*. He really couldn't see 2B going for Thomas Gray. He should have realized that it was a poem that Miss Gilberd herself had had drummed into her at a Girls' High School in the West Riding, sometime in the nineteen-forties. Anyway, she had thrust into his hands a copy of Palgrave's *Golden Treasury*, in its revised and enlarged 1911 edition, prepared and annotated for use in the Public Schools, and he didn't argue. Perhaps, after all, she might have some master plan behind her teaching.

' "Alas! regardless of their doom,
      The little victims play!
No sense have they of ills to come,
      Nor care beyond today . . ." '

'I say, sir,' said Pickerage, looking up at him with his Puck face, 'don't you think that's a bit exaggerated? I mean, schoolboys as little victims, and all that?'

'Oh, I don't know,' said another boy darkly.

'Actually, you've got it a bit wrong,' said Toby. 'What

he's saying is that they play away quite happily, not realizing what's in store for them in the rest of their lives. Though from what I've read about eighteenth-century Eton, anything that came after that could only be a pleasant relief.'

'Was it that bad, sir? Was it worse than here?'

'Of course it was, Pickerage. Infinitely worse.'

'Hilary Frome says that Burleigh is one of the twenty-five worst schools in the country.'

'Then Hilary Frome is talking nonsense. If he thought that he would hardly want to be the next head boy.'

'He said that if the Ministry of Education had any guts, they would refuse to recognize it,' pursued Pickerage.

'He was having you on,' said Toby firmly. And then, slipping out from under this delicate and embarrassing subject, he went on: 'Anyway, you're missing the point, Pickerage. The point is, what is going to happen to these boys *later*. Look, in the very next lines Gray says:

"Yet see, how all around them wait
    The ministers of human fate
And black misfortune's baleful train!"

These are the things that are in store for them in later life.'

'Well,' said Pickerage, obstinately, 'I don't see the ministers of human fate pointing their fingers at me.'

It was a remark that Toby was to remember, with a catch of his breath, a week or so later.

As it happened, Toby was to get a good conspectus that day of the foothills of Burleigh teaching. For after he had supervised lunch, Corbett Farraday came and put his hand on his shoulders and said:

'I say, I'm doing an absolutely top-hole experiment with 4A second period this afternoon. Why don't you come along? It's going to knock them in the aisles.'

He did everything, Toby felt, but say he had a spiffing wheeze. The fact was that Corbett was more than a bit of an embarrassment. He seemed to have got so immovably entrenched in the short trouser stage of life that nothing could ever arouse him to a sense of adult realities. Now he was looking at Toby with the pleading grin of the schoolboy planning a jape, and Toby, who was near enough to that stage to want to put it firmly behind him, would have loved to refuse. But you couldn't refuse Corbett, or speak brutally to him. Somebody should have, perhaps, much earlier in life, but now it was too late.

'I'd love to,' said Toby.

When he came into the labs, Corbett was already poised over a crucible of smoking liquid, looking less like a mad professor than an incompetent short-order cook.

'Now, boys,' he said, 'this should be awfully jolly.'

He waved his hands over the mist-producing crucible, as if he were a Christmas-party conjuror.

'Now, little boys—watch this!'

The little boys—pubescent, sexually precocious fifteen-year-olds—gazed back, some with reluctant expectation, some in tolerance, one with an expression of cultivated languor.

'And now, what do I do? I take this little bottle of the pink stuff . . . and very carefully, very gently, I add it—like this . . .'

He drew, slowly, the little bottle over towards the crucible, seeming to hug himself with anticipation. Nothing delighted him more than to feel twenty-five eyes fixed upon him. Slowly, still like a conjuror, he gently poured a drop or two in. From the crucible there arose a great, green, fluorescent haze, which enveloped the lab bench and the teacher in an inappropriately lurid glow.

'I say,' said Hilary Frome, calculatedly offensive, at the

height of Corbett's triumph, 'do we have to waste time on these party tricks? Some of us want to get through GCE next year, you know.'

Corbett Farraday flinched like a spurned puppy. Toby would have liked to kick Hilary Frome. The trouble was that, as usual, he had a point.

At the end of teaching, the long street towards the centre of Cullbridge was for a time a babble of noise, with scuffles, cap-snatching and schoolboy indecencies hurled from green-blazered groups on one side to green-blazered groups on the other. A sensible quarter of an hour later, the teachers began to trek home, most of them to bachelor quarters of various degrees of chastity. Toby spent some time smoothing the ruffled sensibilities of Corbett Farraday ('I mean, after all, when you *try* to give them a bit of *fun* . . .'), then he went to check the changing huts, which Bill Muggeridge usually forgot to lock after his afternoon tearing round blowing whistles at the boys. Then Toby trudged towards the boarders' annexe which was for the moment his home.

Toby Freely was just nineteen, only a couple of years or so older than the oldest boy at Burleigh. He was the son of a clergyman, and his mother had scrimped and saved and made the lives of her family and parish miserable in order to send her son to Portlington. Portlington was a public school so minor that you got none of the cachet for having been there that is the real point of an English public school education. In fact, you had to go through the humiliating procedure of explaining to everyone that it was indeed a public school. It wasn't much of a place, and Toby hadn't been particularly happy there.

He was in the third-year sixth when he got his place at Trinity Hall, Cambridge. In fact, it was while he was up for the interview that he read in *The Times* the advertisement that had brought him to Burleigh:

GRUBWORTHY AND STING
EDUCATIONAL SERVICES LTD

are seeking for January 1983 SCHOOL LEAVERS to teach games and other subjects in Boys' Private and Preparatory Schools.

No fee whatever is payable for these posts.

The honesty of the advertisement struck him. When he called in at the offices of Grubworthy and Sting, on his way through London, they were no less honest with him.

'Of course, we have to put these advertisements in,' said the tired, courteous, slightly frayed man who interviewed him, 'because we *are* a service for all schools in the private sector. *All* schools, however unsat . . . if you see. But we would hardly recom*mend* . . .'

'I don't know,' said Toby. 'It might suit me. As a fill-in.'

'I mean, look at this one,' said the interviewer, becoming quite indignant and picking one of the schools' letters contemptuously from the pile. ' "Help with games and with the small boarding section. Some elementary teaching in various subjects." My God! They don't want much for nil salary, do they? Lucky they didn't specify they required a Ph.D. "Homely atmosphere." That means the cooking is even more dreadful than it usually is in these places.'

But Toby was made obstinate by his first off-the-cuff effort to get himself a job.

'I think I'd like it,' he said. 'Would I get it?'

'Oh, you'd get it. You don't think there's a queue, do you? But you know, dear boy, the only possible reason for taking a job like this is to get away from school or family.'

'Those are my reasons,' said Toby.

So, having done his best to dissuade him, the man did his best to get him reasonable terms. He threw the name Portlington into the telephone conversation, assured Mr

Crumwallis that it was indeed a Public School, and the results were gratifying. A purr came down the line. Mr Crumwallis even agreed that, in view of his boarding-school duties, Toby should be paid for any teaching he did. In accordance with experience and qualifications. Toby had no experience or qualifications.

He had taken up his duties shortly after the beginning of the spring term, when he was sure of his place at Trinity Hall. The school had fulfilled all the worst forebodings of the gentleman at Grubworthy and Sting, but Toby had not been unhappy. He had more or less sole charge of the twenty-seven boys in the boarding section. One evening off a week he had insisted on, and on those evenings Mr or Mrs Crumwallis occasionally poked their noses through into the boarding annexe and yelled 'Shut up' through the riot proceeding there. Otherwise Toby was father, mother and elder brother to the boys, and on the whole he enjoyed himself, creating for them the home he felt he had never had himself. Many of the boys were children of army families, or business families settled abroad. They were mostly a little lonely and disorientated, enjoying none of the (few) advantages of the ordinary boarding-school, and too few in number to feel any sense of corporate identity. Toby felt he was doing good.

Today he trudged up to his cubbyhole of a room, showered in the communal bathroom, and went along to tea at four-thirty. Tea was a plate of doorsteps cut by Mrs Garfitt the housekeeper at one-thirty, as soon as school lunch was over. If the doorsteps could have curled at the edges, they would have done so. She had regarded his suggestion that they be put in plastic as a piece of impertinence to a woman of her years.

'Oh God, raspberry jam again,' said Mortimer, as he entered the room. 'Toby, why is it always raspberry jam?'

They called him Toby in the boarding annexe, 'sir' in

the school, except when they got it mixed up.

'It isn't always raspberry,' said Toby. 'I distinctly remember fish paste last Thursday.'

'Ugh, filthy old fish paste.'

'Look at this fruit cake,' said Pickerage, the live wire of the boarding annexe. 'It must be months old. All dry and crumbly.'

'Nonsense, it's perfectly all right. Meant to be like that.'

'My mother never makes cakes that are meant to be dry and crumbly,' said Mortimer.

'Hilary Frome says he sees old Garfitt round the back door of the baker's on her way to school in the mornings,' chimed in Pickerage. 'Buying up all the really old stuff for practically nothing. I expect it's true, don't you, Toby?'

'No, I don't. And why are you quoting Hilary Frome every other sentence these days, Pickerage? Doesn't anyone else ever say anything worth remembering?'

'Not really. Anyway, he's my friend. He often talks to me. We're good friends, Hilary and I.'

Pickerage said it self-importantly. Hilary Frome was, after all, head boy designate. But in Toby's experience friendship between a boy in his fourth year and one in his second was a rare occurrence, and one which would usually be a particular sort of friendship.

Toby decided to keep his eye on Hilary Frome.

CHAPTER 3

PARENTS' EVENING

There was one thing, Toby thought, about Mr Crum-wallis: the teachers might dislike or despise him, but in the end they toed his line. Like tonight, Parents' Evening,

when they had assembled at his behest in the Staff
Common Room overlooking the school driveway to watch
out for arriving parents and usher them through to the
headmaster's sitting-room, where the first part of the
festivities were to take place. Or was it less his personality
that accounted for their compliance than his power—a
power so much greater than that of a headmaster within
the State system? Glenda Grower, who rarely commented
on her past career within that system, seemed to think so.

'And so, my children,' she said, dominating the staff
room as inevitably she dominated whenever she chose, 'so
we all troop along an hour early, as commanded by the
Great God Crumwallis, to usher the parents from their
Daimlers and along to the glittering scene awaiting them
in the Crumwallis quarters. Aren't we good little
children? Or are we, perhaps, merely craven? We have,
after all, a meagre enough amount of free time. It
wouldn't have happened, I can tell you, at Bedfordshire
Comprehensive.'

Glenda Grower's hair, auburn and shiny, was normally
tied in a neat bun at the back of her head, but tonight it
had been allowed to stream glamorously down her back.
She had been at one of the best State schools in England,
where she would still be, no doubt, but for what Toby
had heard referred to as an Incident. Toby would have
liked to inquire further, but had feared a snub at his age
and inexperience. It accounted, he supposed, for her
aloofness, and the occasional appearance of resentment
and unhappiness.

'Not all of us are toeing the line,' said Tom Tedder.
'McWhirter's not here, for one.'

'But then, our Mr McWhirter's a law unto himself, is
he not?' said Glenda, tossing a splendid lock back from
over her eye. 'No doubt he will shuffle in five minutes
after the first parent comes, and shuffle out half an hour
before the last one goes. Money talks.'

'Don't underestimate him,' said Septimus Coffin, tugging at his tufty moustache. 'He may be the world's most tedious teacher and its driest personality, but he has one admirable quality: he is totally honest. When Mrs Whatsit asks him tonight why her little Johnny isn't making more progress with his English, Iain McWhirter will reply that progress is not to be expected from a boy who is abysmally lazy and congenitally stupid.'

'Whereas the rest of us,' said Glenda Grower, 'will mutter something like "perhaps his real strengths do lie elsewhere".'

'It seems a good idea,' said Penny Warlock, looking up to Glenda and wondering if she herself would be as impressive a figure after ten or fifteen years in the teaching profession. 'Perhaps I'll try the total honesty line.'

'I *wouldn't*,' said Glenda Grower. 'I really wouldn't. But bully for McWhirter. As I say, money is power.'

'I don't think it's anything to do with money,' said Septimus Coffin. 'It's his position as licensed eccentric. Though, mind you, it scares the pants off poor old Crumwallis. Watch him tonight. He'll be on tenterhooks the whole time, and muttering to the parents things like: "A true eccentric, our Mr McWhirter, but a very fine scholar in his field." '

'Anyway,' said Toby, 'he's not the only absentee. Bill Muggeridge hasn't pitched up yet.'

'The Crumwallises would very much rather he didn't pitch up at all,' said Glenda. 'They don't feel he gives the place tone. The awful thing is that one almost agrees. I do rather object to the sort of chap who farts in public and then says "Better out than in." '

'He said earlier,' chirrupped little Mr Makepeace, 'that Onyx was insisting on coming.'

'Oh my God—it only needed that. Just introducing her is an embarrassment. On what grounds would she be coming?'

'Well, Muggeridge said she was complaining he never takes her anywhere. And she *has* taught with us now and then.'

'Fill-in hours. She's about the only person that even Crumwallis is reluctant to employ. Normally he's quite happy to go out and grab someone from the street. I say, look: a parent.'

And indeed a car—not a Daimler, but a puce Ford Fiesta—had coasted down the drive.

'A parent,' repeated Glenda. 'Anybody know it? They can take it through to the ancestral ballroom.'

'Oh—it looks—yes—it's the Wevewent Martins,' said Mr Makepeace, who knew all the vicars, rectors, rural deans and curates in a twenty-mile radius. 'He's the vicar of Bwimstone Parva.'

'Ah, well, since you know him . . .'

'He's awfully *low*—church, I mean.'

'Could you,' said Glenda sweetly, 'just perhaps *bend* a little for once?'

But as Percy Makepeace twittered through the hall and down the corridor with his clerical acquaintance, two more cars drew up in the Burleigh driveway. One by one the teachers squared their shoulders and assumed the burden of the festivities.

By eight-thirty the headmaster's sitting-room was nicely full. Fifty or sixty parents were present, and were talking in nervous or gushing little groups which centred on one or other of the teachers. Mr McWhirter had shuffled in, looking like a morose vagrant, some ten minutes late, and had taken up a position in front of the fire. Only the bolder or more totally disillusioned parents braved his forthright opinions of their sons and heirs. More regrettably still, Bill Muggeridge arrived, looking what he was—an ex-fourth-division footballer: bulky, grubby, in an unbrushed suit and with a button missing from his shirt. In tow was the equally regrettable Onyx. How she had got that name no one dared ask. To give it to a child would seem unnaturally insensitive; to assume it oneself would argue a capacity for self-inflicted wounds beyond even Onyx's nature. She was a dreary, promiscuous, disorganized piece of human driftwood, who kept having babies of dubious provenance. She slouched from parent to parent, latching on to those who looked as if they would listen to her woes—not realizing, perhaps, that this was hardly the purpose of Parents' Evening.

Most of the parents, however, had come intending to talk about their boys, either out of a genuine or an assumed interest in them; and few of them were prepared to waste time on Onyx when there were real teachers on whom to vent their parental concern.

'James is such a *sensitive* little boy,' the Rev. Martins was saying to Glenda Grower, 'and so easily discouraged. He has to be tempted to learn.'

'Yes,' said Glenda, noncommittally. 'Certainly he doesn't give the impression that history is where his main interest lies.'

'Frank's never going to be more than your average brain,' said Major Tilney to Toby Freely. 'In the old days they'd have thumped enough into him to get him through his exam. I suppose you have to find some other method. The main thing is, he seems happier this term as a boarder.'

'Yes, he does seem to be settling down well,' said Toby Freely. 'It's small enough to have a sort of family atmosphere.'

'Hmmph,' said Major Tilney. 'I don't see the headmaster and his wife as homemakers, to be brutally frank. But from what I can gather from his scrawls you're doing a good job.'

'He's a boy,' said Mrs Cantribb, greatly daring, to Mr McWhirter, knowing very well the nature of his teaching methods, 'who responds to *stimulus*.'

'He's a numbskull,' said Mr McWhirter witheringly. 'You can't stimulate when there's nothing there to respond.'

The headmaster, who had just finished dispensing multi-racial condescension to Mr Patel and was now turning gratefully to Dr and Mrs Frome, gazed with ill-disguised apprehension in the direction of Mr McWhirter.

'Every school should have its eccentrics,' he said, bravely. 'We are fortunate that ours is a man of genuine, first-rate scholarship.'

Dr and Mrs Frome looked at Mr McWhirter as if not entirely convinced. Then they turned to the headmaster and launched into the topic all three of them had closest to their hearts: the Fromes' only son.

The Fromes were certainly among the smartest parents present that evening, though in no ostentatious way. They were, like their son, smooth. Dr Frome was in his forties, with a clean-cut profile and the remains of Rupert Brooke good looks. His decisive, no-nonsense manner had given him the reputation of being a good doctor, and this had been only slightly dented by one or two spectacularly wrong diagnoses. His wife was also handsome—blonde, tactfully made-up, with a figure and face preserved by hard work and frequent attendance at beauty specialists. There was a slight gush in her manner which gave the impression that she was the stupider of the two. The impression was wrong. If Dr Frome had not been stupid, he would not have sent his son, of whom he thought a lot, to a school like Burleigh. Snobbery had fought with economy, and the two had reached a very silly compromise.

'Of course, as you know, Hilary did want to transfer to the Comprehensive for his GCE year,' said Mrs Frome.

'But we're delighted at the thought of his being head boy here.'

'I know he's going to do a first-rate job,' said Edward Crumwallis, gazing towards the door, where Hilary Frome was already doing a first-rate job with two of the more important parents.

'Nevertheless, there *are* still the GCEs,' said Dr Frome. 'And Hilary's strengths are on the mathematics/scientific sides (as my own were). I want to have a good talk with Mr Makepeace and Mr Farraday . . .'

There seemed the suspicion of an implied threat here that Mr Crumwallis did not at all like.

'He couldn't be in better hands,' he said, spuriously confident. 'Makepeace has a first from Reading, you know.' (How he wished he could have said Oxford. Still, it was close.) 'Top-class chap in his field. Hilary couldn't have a better coach for GCE Maths.'

'There's the question of discipline . . .' said Dr Frome.

Similar preoccupations were at the back of the mind of Hilary Frome himself, as, with the front of his mind, he made conversation with the overdressed parents of one of the boarders. Hilary Frome had made no decisions yet about his future, beyond the one crucial decision that it was going to be a distinguished one. He was going to make a splash — the nature of which was still to be determined. An obvious possibility was an academic splash, and throughout his years at Burleigh he had chafed at the mediocrity of the school, the variable nature of the teaching, the dimness of its reputation, all of which seemed to preclude the splash academic. Of course, if he settled for Burleigh for one more year, there was the position of head boy, with all the possibilities for mischief of a sophisticated and enticing sort that that would bring with it. But at what cost! Still, it was as well not to close off any possibility of future splash, so he stood there, in his immaculate green blazer and flannels, his tie neatly knotted, his profile presented most becomingly to Mr and Mrs Channing, as he acted the role of head boy in some long-forgotten boys' book by Talbot Baines Reed or Annesley Vachell.

'Tommy's soccer is improving enormously,' he said at random, having no idea, nor caring, whether this was true or not.

'Oh, really?' said the heavily over-painted Mrs Channing. 'He always says he doesn't care for the game. Of course, Tommy is an awfully sensitive little boy.'

Sensitivity, be it noted, was the quality most often claimed for their offspring by the parents in the course of their conversations and consultations that evening. With the unpredictability of fashion, it seems that sensitivity has replaced brains or athletic ability as the quality all boys should aim at. Certainly, if they were to be believed, Burleigh was a positive hot-house of delicate blossoms.

'Oh yes, I think all of us here can see that, Mrs Channing,' said Hilary Frome.

'One would have *shuddered* to send him to a public school,' said the lady, who had in fact sat long and agonized in calculation of the cost of doing so. 'But we decided the boarding section at Burleigh was so *small*—like a large, warm family. It sounded such a friendly place—'

'Oh, it is. Awfully friendly,' said Hilary Frome.

'Tommy does need a little *love*,' said Mrs Channing.

Hilary Frome gave the most tremendous inward smirk.

'I think you can rely on his getting it,' he said. 'Would you be so kind as to excuse me for a moment? I have to go and supervise the refreshments.'

In the large kitchen off the sitting-room Mrs Crumwallis was organizing in no very effective manner the refreshment of the masses. She peered closely at the surrounding mass of faces, comprising ten of the cleaner or nicer-looking boys from the boarding section, who were whispering and fooling among themselves and taking little notice of her. She went over the points for the tenth time.

'Two biscuits on each saucer,' she said in her crow-like voice. 'Go and ask them what they want, then ask them if they want milk and sugar with it, then ask another one the same, and then come back here and get two cups and the biscuits from me. Is that clear?'

'Yes, Mrs Crumwallis,' said the ragged chorus.

'I think they know what's to be done, Mrs Crumwallis,' said Hilary Frome, coming in from the sitting-room and taking immediate charge. 'Pickerage, you start with the parents in the far corner by the door. Tilney, you take the parents around the fireplace. Wattling—you take the ones by the occasional table . . .'

Efficiently the boys were sped on their various errands. Mrs Crumwallis poised herself over her urns in her favourite position, while Hilary Frome acted on Milton's assurance that they also served who only stood and waited.

'It's just my luck,' said Onyx Muggeridge to Major Tilney in her plaintive tones, the whine of the professionally put-upon. 'Men always turn out like that in my life—the ones I'm interested in. I mean, look at Bill—there he was, a footballer with Colchester, a league side, the world all before him. You'd have thought it couldn't go wrong, wouldn't you? And now look at him. The original no-where man. The trouble with me is, I'm too trusting.'

She took the Major's arm confidingly. Used as he had been in his youth to the drabs of the garrison towns, the Major nevertheless began courteously to disengage himself.

'Tea or coffee, sir?'

The interruption of young Pickerage, looking up

elfishly, was welcome to the Major.

'Oh, er — is that the choice?'

'Pretty much, sir. Oh — there is some fruit cup out there.'

'Well, I've never been one for tea or coffee after seven o'clock. I'll see what the fruit cup's like.'

As the cups and saucers were brought round, teachers and parents began to circulate. Dorothea Gilberd edged away from the parents to whom she had been uttering words of reassurance about their little Philip's future and glided quite at random in the direction of Tom Tedder.

'Look at her,' said Onyx Muggeridge spitefully. 'The human equivalent of cling plastic.'

The Major began to feel that Onyx Muggeridge was not quite what he had come to a parents' evening for, and was quite grateful when the headmaster disengaged himself with palpable reluctance from the Fromes and sailed in his direction, exuding Manner.

'Ah, Major Tilney. Boys getting you something, I trust? I can recommend the tea. Thoroughly recommend it.'

'Wouldn't know one tea from another. He's getting me some fruit cup stuff.'

'Ah — good. We made that up for the boys, but if you prefer . . .' neighed Mr Crumwallis, congratulating himself on insisting on something that at least looked a bit special.

And certainly, when the Major sipped his, he was surprised at how palatable it was.

While the meagre refreshments were doled out, or refills were procured, the little groups around the teachers began to break up, and the whole occasion gradually became more flexible. Parent began to talk to parent.

'I hear from Tommy,' said Mrs Channing, gazing significantly in the direction of Glenda Grower, 'that she's an *awfully* good history teacher. Burleigh is terribly lucky to have her.'

'Place needs all the good teachers it can get, from what I can gather,' said Major Tilney.

'It's the salary they pay. And of course we wouldn't want the fees higher, would we? The only reason they could get Miss Grower on the staff was that Incident at her previous school, you know . . .''

'Incident? What kind of Incident?'

'I really wouldn't like to be more specific. Let's just say that she's quite safe in a *boys'* school . . .'

Lesbianism held no terrors for the Major, who had long experience of the women's services. He drained his glass to the dregs, and felt a pleasant, warming, unmistakable sensation rising to his cheeks.

'I'll have another one of those, young feller-me-lad,' he said to Pickerage, who was passing.

The headmaster saw the mingling of parents, unchaperoned by teachers, with distaste. A dangerous development: parents left alone were apt to swap causes of dissatisfaction with the school. Already, he could hear, the Major and Mrs Channing had progressed from Glenda Grower to some of the deficiencies of the boarding establishment. It was time to break things up. He joined Mr McWhirter, standing by the fire in the usual lonely state of the one honest man, and, assuming his Manner at its most impressive, he cleared his throat.

'Errgh.'

The room fell silent, and from his great height he gazed over the room with that familiar expression he put on when being headmasterly — an expression that was at once dyspeptic yet predatory (for were they not, after all, his prey?).

'It is — ah — splendid and — ah — heartwarming to see you all here enjoying yourselves, and I want to say—ah—how much pleasure it gives my good wife and—ah—myself' (he could never work out whether it should be 'I' or 'me') 'to be able to entertain you in our modest home. But we have business to be done, too, tonight, and I know that many of you are anxious to have a chat to the—ah—instructors of your boys. And I know they are hoping to have a talk to you, too, because all of us here at Burleigh realize how important it is to get a—ah—total picture of the child, of his problems, his hopes, his ambitions, his—ah—ah— Hmmm. Now, Miss Gilberd, our valued teacher of the lower forms, will be in classroom 2B to talk to anybody who might wish to go along and see her; Mr Makepeace will be in 4A; Mr Farraday in the scientific laboratories, of course; Mr Coffin in 5B . . .'

As the recital proceeded, the teachers began to drift off to their appointed confessional boxes, anxious to miss, on any excuse, as much as possible of the headmaster's address.

'And if you cannot find the room you want,' Mr Crumwallis concluded, 'I know that Hilary Frome, our valued head boy for the next year, will be happy to show you the way.'

He gestured towards the door, where Hilary Frome was standing, flaunting his fair hair and profile, and looking still more like an illustration of one of Baden Powell's scouting manuals; a fine specimen of British boyhood, who in only a matter of a year or two might be imagined assuming the burden of Empire, and administering imperial justice with rod and gun to one or other of the lesser breeds without the law.

'And—ah—I shall be in my study, and delighted to meet any of you, should you care to come along for a chat,' said the headmaster, very much as an afterthought, and clearly hoping they wouldn't.

It was while the assembly was breaking up, and parents

and staff were drifting to their various meeting points, that Major Tilney heard distinctly, through the closed door to the kitchen, a high-pitched hiccup and an outbreak of hysterical boyish laughter.

Mrs Crumwallis paused in the piling up of cups and saucers and the conserving of uneaten biscuits (so generously supplied by Miss Gilberd) for future boarders' teas. She squinted in bewilderment at the ten or so boarders who had formed her little band of helpers. A quarter of an hour ago they had been more than a little discontented. When they had sampled her hastily flung-together fruit cup she had distinctly registered — for her hearing was as acute as her eyesight was bad — mutterings of distaste and dissatisfaction.

'Ugh, what beastly muck,' Wattling had said.

'It's all bitter,' young Tilney had exclaimed.

Now the discontented group had been transformed into the merriest little gang of kids since the first night of *Oliver*. The centre of the group was Wattling, perched on a chair surrounded by his admiring peers, and attempting to sing 'Doh, a deer, a female deer' — revealing, in the attempt, conspicuous deficiencies in his knowledge of the tonic sol-fa.

'I say,' said Pickerage, coming in from the sitting-room.

'I say, I say, I say,' shouted Wattling in response, switching to his music hall routine.

'Old Major Tilney just slipped me half a quid,' said Pickerage. 'What do you think he did that for?'

'Perhaps he fancied you,' said Broughton, the oldest boy, his face flushed a bright, livid pink.

'Watch it,' said Tilney. 'He *is* my dad.'

'If I was your dad I'd fancy anyone — *hic* — rather than you,' said Martins. 'I say, Pickerage, have some of the fruit cup. It tastes funny, but when you get used to it, it isn't half bad.'

'You boys are *supposed* to be helping with the washing up,' said Mrs Crumwallis, in the tones of an aggrieved crow. 'Look lively. Wattling, bring me those saucers there.'

Wattling turned uncertainly to the table, took up cautiously the pile of saucers, and started with them waveringly to the sink. Before he got half way, they dropped with an almighty crash on to the stone floor. A delighted howl of laughter went up, drowning the eldritch shriek of Mrs Crumwallis.

'I say, Wattling — *hic* — you've dropped the saucers.'

'You are a clot — what?'

'Boys!'

'Try again, Wattling. There's another pile.'

'Bet you can't get them to the sink, Wattling.'

'You can't walk straight, Wattling.'

'Yes, I can, see. I tripped.'

'BOYS!'

'Go on, Wattling, pick 'em up.'

'I say, Wattling can't find the saucers. He can't see properly.'

'Can, see. They're *there*.'

'Good old Wattling. Bet you can't walk straight with them.'

'Go it, Wattling.'

'BOYS!'

It was at the height of the disorder that the noise penetrated to Toby Freely. He was the last to leave the sitting-room, calculating that the parents of boarders would talk to the regular teachers before coming along to talk to him. The giggling was usual enough, but the quality of it was not normal, and it augmented itself to laughter that was even more hysterical, then to delirious *hics*, and jeering shouts. The sound puzzled him: it was wrong for boys in the presence of Mrs Crumwallis. And when he heard the first crash he determined to intervene, in some way that would not dispute the authority of the headmaster's wife. By the time he had worked out how to do this the riot had increased, and he was forced to fling open the door.

Crash. Another pile of saucers went.

'Mr Freely!' shrieked Mrs Crumwallis. 'They've gone mad! I can't do anything with them!'

'They're not mad, Mrs Crumwallis. They're drunk.'

'Drunk? Nonsense. They've only had my fruit cup.'

'Sir! Toby!' yelled a boy. 'Look at Tilney. He's going to spew.'

And Tilney, leaning greenly over the kitchen table, began with a spectacular heave to do just that.

'See to him, Mrs Crumwallis,' yelled Toby. 'I'll get this lot out. The parents can't see them like this.'

And grabbing three of the smallest around their necks, he started pushing them out of the back door, into the fresh air, and towards the outer door of the boarding section.

'Right—follow them,' he commanded the rest. 'Broughton, I'm surprised at you. Don't make so much *noise*. Go to the outer door and then go up to the dorms, but do it *quietly*. I'm right behind you, but you mustn't let the parents hear. *Quiet*, you there . . .'

It was as he was shepherding the tail end out that the headmaster made a belated appearance.

'Freely!' he fumed. 'What is this deplorable disturbance? Get those boys back to the dormitories at once.'

For the headmaster, pusillanimous in action, was always ready to follow up the action of others.

Major Tilney, when he left the main block of Burleigh, lit a cigarette as he walked down the drive to the road. He had expected to have a little chat with his boy, but the headmaster had explained that he had been put to bed early because he had an important French test the next day.

The Major had not been deceived. He knew that boys of twelve did not have French tests so important as to prevent their seeing their fathers. He knew there had been alcohol in the fruit cup, and plenty of it. He had heard the hiceups from the kitchen. The boys had got drunk.

He enjoyed the thought hugely. It reminded him of his boyhood reading. It wouldn't do the kids any harm. He was in Cullbridge for the night, and he'd see his lad in the morning. He'd be willing to bet he'd be as bleary as hell. He smiled again. No harm in it. Damned good jape. No harm in it at all.

The headmaster thought otherwise. He said so to his wife when everyone had finally gone home. He took the matter very seriously indeed. It was an outrage, and somebody was going to pay. If it hadn't been for his quick-mindedness, he said, goodness knows what scandal might not have ensued. He intended to regard it as an incident of the utmost gravity.

And though the Major was a man of very much greater intelligence than the headmaster, it was in this case, for once in his life, Mr Crumwallis who was in the right.

CHAPTER 4

BOYS

The life of the boarding annexe next day was dominated by ten young boys with horrendous hangovers. Such pains and miseries as they did not feel, they acted out: acting, indeed, at this level of ham had not been seen since the last World Cup, or the Peter O'Toole *Macbeth*. The act was performed with particular virtuosity when Mrs Crumwallis dosed them all with castor oil, an old-fashioned cure-all in which she had a fiendish trust: then the boys' performance resembled nothing so much as an acted-out illustration for *Nicholas Nickleby*. Toby Freely felt somewhat out of his depth, not confident enough to sort out the genuine from the assumed. The ten boys were patently enjoying their notoriety, though, and after lunch-time Toby decided that sympathy had better give way to a brisk, enough-of-this approach if the boarding block was ever to return to normal. With such a sure-fire topic for reminiscence and speculation, however, this was far from easy to achieve.

Mr Crumwallis, inevitably, conducted what he described as a 'rigorous inquiry'. Equally inevitably, it got nowhere. He had none of the equipment of a detective, neither being particularly observant nor having any great insight into the psychology of small boys. In the end he slippered Pickerage and called it a day. His action was unfavourably commented on in the Staff Common Room. As Septimus Coffin pointed out: if he had really thought Pickerage had done it, he would have caned him; if he didn't know whether he had done it or not, he shouldn't have slippered him.

Later one of the day boys, on his way home after being kept in, saw an empty bottle of Smirnoff's in the long grass near the drive. After some consideration he kicked it still further into the undergrowth.

By Friday evening Toby Freely congratulated himself that the boarding block was beginning to return to normal. The boarding annexe at Burleigh was an unlovely square built on to the main house in the nineteen-twenties — it was the cause, in fact, of the original owner going bankrupt and being forced to forsake the licensed trade. The main part of the school was considerably more attractive, being a red-brick residence, rambling but characterful, built for the vendor of wine and spirits in the last years of the Old Queen, when people were beginning to wonder if she would ever go. Situated on the outskirts of Cullbridge, it was reached by a long drive edged by trees and shrubs. The front part of the house, being somewhat darkened by evergreens, was given over to the Staff Common Room, with the classrooms of the senior forms on the first floor. The back part of the house, being lighter and pleasanter and giving out on to the lawn, was the headmaster's residence. There were also some additional classrooms, built on in the 'forties, when building controls were strict and architectural standards were low: this extension was a long, straight line of jerry-built square rooms, projecting from the right of the original house.

The boarding annexe had its own outside door, leading towards the headmaster's lawn, where the boys sometimes played (*quietly*, of course, insisted Mr Crumwallis) on spring evenings. It also had a door leading into the main house, connecting with the headmaster's hall, whence Mr Crumwallis made his occasional incursions. On the ground floor of the annexe there was a large room where the boarders, and those day boys who took it, ate school lunch (it was called dinner at the Cullbridge Comprehensive, but lunch at Burleigh—which somewhat excused the meagreness of it, though not the high price charged for it). Above were the boarders' dormitories, a recreation room or two, the sick bay (only one boy was allowed to be sick at a time) and a small bedroom for Toby. It was not a comfortable environment for the boarders, but its very shabbiness made it liveable in.

The routine of the annexe on Friday after school was disturbed by Mr Crumwallis making ineffectual invasions of it from time to time. He had been alarmed by the narrowly-averted disaster of the previous evening, and felt the need to assert his presence.

'All present and correct?' he would demand of Toby, or 'What are the boys doing now?' Eventually his little spurt of concern subsided, and he collapsed in front of the television in his own quarters, engrossed in a long-running J. B. Priestley serial.

'I feel better now,' said young Tilney to Toby, as the boys sat around eating supper — a potato pie that Mrs Garfitt had left for them, and which Toby had put in the oven. 'Do you think I might eventually get a taste for alcohol?'

'I've no doubt you will,' said Toby. 'But do you mind trying not to get it just yet?'

'Toby,' said Wattling, shovelling in a forkful, 'who do you think did it?'

There was no point in asking what *it* was. There was only one topic of conversation at Burleigh that evening.

'The headmaster,' said Toby carefully, 'decided that Pickerage must have done it.'

Pickerage let out an exaggerated groan.

'Well, I didn't. I've had alcohol before, and I don't like it. I know what it does to you, and I don't want to feel like I feel now, thanks very much. Anyway, the head didn't really think I did it.'

' 'Course he did,' said Hoddnett, one of the older boys. 'Otherwise he wouldn't have slippered you.'

'He slippered me because there had to be someone slippered. But he didn't slipper hard.'

'You yelled like a stuck pig.'

'Of course I did. That's part of the game. But he didn't slipper hard. Personally,' he added, saying that word in a very considered and grown-up manner, 'I think one of the teachers did it.'

'What nonsense, Pickerage,' said Toby firmly. 'They weren't even around the kitchen.'

'Well, they were — see. Several of them. Before they

went through to the staff room to take up positions when the parents arrived. And Miss Gilberd and that awful Muggeridge always come through the back, because it's the quickest way from their homes. Muggeridge and his soppy wife were in there for ages on their way through—she was ear-bashing Mrs Crumwallis.'

'And the Grower went back to get herself another cup of coffee,' said Wattling, 'though *we* were supposed to do that.'

'I bet it was one of the Muggeridges,' said Tilney.

'What absolute bilge, Tilney,' said Toby, forced into solidarity with one of his least favourite fellow members of staff. 'Why on earth would either of them do a thing like that?'

'He's a spiteful bugger,' said Wattling. 'You never played footer with him, Toby. I expect he just wanted to make us very ill.'

'Rubbish. If he'd got a down on you, he could get back at you any time he wanted.'

'Perhaps *she* did it, to get him into a jolly big row. So that he had to get a job elsewhere—somewhere much better,' said Pickerage.

Toby tried to see Onyx as an Eton gamesmaster's wife. He failed. He looked at his watch.

'Come on. Time for bed for the young ones.'

The young ones, as always, made a frightful racket as they got ready for bed. The whole thing was a sort of ritual, with the same motions performed night after night. Tilney always managed to make the business of cleaning one's teeth sound like an electric drill demolishing part of the Barbican, while Wattling's idea of washing his face was to chuck his flannel at it and spatter water all over the bathroom. Wattling's father was in the army, and his mother spent half of the year in Singapore or wherever he happened to be stationed, so his state was even more bereft than Tilney's, whose parents were divorced but whose father was stationed less than fifty miles away. Pickerage had a mother somewhere or other, who liked to descend on the school at inopportune moments, always driving a different car, the property of her current escort (she was the sort of woman who, even in this day and age, had escorts), and embarrassing Pickerage by the demonstrable falsity of her pretended affection. Toby prided himself that at the moment none of these boys, or the two dozen others, was conspicuously unhappy.

When they had got into bed, it was Toby's custom to read them a chapter or two of a book—the school had a tattered library of elderly boys' books, most of them left behind by ex-pupils. Luckily boys don't notice datedness too readily, and the boarders seemed to lap up Biggles, or John Buchan, or even Edgar Wallace. Tonight, though, they were all too excited to be read to.

'I'll tell you what Hilary Frome says about—'

There was a general groan against Pickerage, in which Toby gladly joined.

'No, shut up, let me tell you,' said Pickerage. 'After all, he should know.'

'Why should he know?' said Toby. 'Put a sock in it, Pickerage. I'm sure the boy doesn't want to be quoted as if he was a cross between the *Encyclopaedia Britannica* and the Authorized Version.'

'He knows all about this school,' said Pickerage obstinately. 'And he says old Coffin and McWhirter would like to take over Burleigh. Get out the Crumwallises and run it themselves. He says it was probably old Coffin.'

'Well, one thing I know about Mr Coffin is that he was born in the early nineteen-twenties. That makes him over sixty. Can you really imagine anyone hatching a devious plot to take over the school at his age?'

'I don't see why not,' said Tilney, who was at the age

when the more outrageous the idea, the better. 'They say the population is getting older and older, so he probably has years to go yet.'

'Anyway—that's enough speculation for tonight, right?' said Toby, getting up. 'And enough Hilary Frome.'

He shouldn't have mentioned the name.

'Hilary's taking me home on Sunday,' said Pickerage, fighting against sleep. 'He's going to introduce me to his parents. And he's going to teach me to play squash.'

Is he, by God? thought Toby, firmly switching off the light.

Later that evening, when he was playing a desultory game of Scrabble with Broughton and Hoddnett, two of the older boys, he casually brought the subject up.

'We really get our fill of Hilary Frome from young Pickerage at the moment,' he said.

The two boys laughed blandly, giving nothing away.

'Hilary's the great man in this school these days,' said Hoddnett. 'Every great man has to have disciples.'

'I wish him luck of Pickerage,' said Toby. 'Personally I'd feel safer with Judas Iscariot.'

The two laughed, but they loosened up a little.

'He's a bright lad, Pickerage,' said Broughton. 'Lively. Up to anything.'

'That's what I'm afraid of,' said Toby. 'I don't want this Frome leading him into trouble.'

'Oh, Hilary wouldn't do that,' said Broughton. 'Hilary's a smart operator. He keeps within the limits.'

'His limits,' said Hoddnett.

Earlier that day, when school had ended at a quarter to four, Hilary Frome had walked down the long road towards Cullbridge with Willis and Quigly. Quigly, Willis and Frome—it would have formed a sufficiently high-sounding trio of names to grace a solicitors' firm. And indeed the fathers of all three boys were professional men, filling positions of trust or responsibility, and ones bringing a degree of social prestige. They all belonged to golf clubs or sailing clubs, took their holidays abroad, and were devoted Masons; two of them had stood for the local council. Like clings to like, and in so far as Hilary Frome had friends of his own age—mostly he had followers—those friends were Willis and Quigly.

As they walked along, weaving through the little groups of fighting or jesting juniors, the three boys were discussing what they were to do over the weekend.

'I'm going swimming on Saturday,' said Willis, in an assumedly bored voice that was modelled on Hilary's. 'My dad's all enthusiastic about swimming, God knows why. Times me, and hands over a quid when I cut a fraction of a second off my record—can you imagine? Then I suppose I'll go to that disco over at Hadleigh. Everyone seems to be going.'

'All the more reason for *not*,' said Hilary Frome. 'All those sweaty bodies . . .'

'I didn't know you had anything against sweaty bodies,' said Quigley. 'Won't you be there, then?'

'Margaret wants me to go with her,' said Hilary, with a languid gesture. 'Perhaps that's another reason for not going.'

'Tired of the heterosexual kick, Hilary?' asked Quigly.

'Nothing remains a kick long, does it?' said Hilary, scooping back a lock of fair hair from over his eye. 'And one sees so much of the hetero thing at school: the Gilberd mooning after Tedder; Billy Bunter Farraday mooning after little Penny; sweet little Toby mooning after little Penny . . .'

'Makes a change from la Grower mooning after little Penny,' said Willis, and they all laughed.

'Well, I hope she wins,' said Hilary. 'One does get so sick of the normal and the expected.'

'Then you'd better keep away from the disco,' said Willis. 'If there ever was anywhere given over to the normal and the expected, it's a disco at Hadleigh.'

'I expect I'll give it a miss,' said Hilary. 'Weep your eyes out, Margaret. In any case, I have this date with Pickerage on Sunday.'

The other two laughed.

'That's more our Hilary,' said Willis.

'Better make your mind up,' said Quigly. 'Get yourself sorted out.'

'Sorted out? Do you have to sound like the *vicar*, Quigly? I see no reason why I should sort myself out. The world is over-stocked with sorted out people.'

'And what is your line?'

'Me? I sample. I savour. I roll the flavour of the month round in my mouth. I flit from flower to flower, and I pick up different things from different flowers.'

'Bully for you. And what is the flitting bee going to do on his date with Pickerage?'

'Really, Willis, mind your own business. I'm not even sure that I've decided yet.'

'After that write-up, it had better be something a bit more decisive than tossing each other off in the bogs.'

'What a crude, Sunday paper mind you have, Willis. And what makes you think I choose Pickerage to toss me off in the bogs?'

'You asked to go spot on half past two in Makepeace's class today. I'm by the window and I'd seen Pickerage make his enticing little way there just a minute before. You arranged it.'

'You have a very narrow range of ideas as to what can be done with Pickerage in the bog. If I want that, there's ten or twelve in his year I'd fancy more. Wattling, for example. Actually Pickerage and I have a relationship that goes much deeper than your grubby little mind could encompass, Quigly.'

'All that means is that he's your latest disciple.'

'Disciple? Is that what you think, Quigly? Of course, he would make a very good successor.'

'You haven't gone yet.'

'Well, this year, next year—it won't be long. And without me the school might sink into torpor. Passive acceptance would be the order of the day. This school is too awful to deserve passive acceptance. There has to be someone around to galvanize you lot into action.'

'Is *that* all you're planning to do with Pickerage on Sunday? Train him up in the role of *agent provocateur?*'

'Really, Willis, your French accent is quite ghastly. Anyone'd think you'd never been south of Harwich. Actually, I haven't decided what I'm going to be doing with Pickerage on Sunday. But I think it'd better be something original, something with a bit of spice. Because I admit that I'm bored, and that's unforgivable. I'd hate to think I was going stale.'

Hilary said the same thing, in a rather different tone of voice, over the breakfast table next morning to his parents.

'I think I'll be away most of the day tomorrow,' he said. 'I feel like a long hike somewhere or other.'

'A good Sunday walk is always a good thing,' said Mrs Frome.

'I'll do something a bit longer than that,' said Hilary. 'Take some food and be away the whole day. All this responsibility at school is getting on top of me. I can feel myself going stale. And if I'm going to be head boy, I can't afford to get stale.'

They looked at him, fondly and proudly. When he'd got up and gone out, Dr Frome said to his wife:

'I think after all it was a good plan to keep Hilary at Burleigh. In spite of the academic standards. That boy is showing a real sense of responsibility these days.'

CHAPTER 5

TEACHERS

It needed no especial acuteness of perception in Hilary Frome to discover that Penny Warlock was the axle around which the sexual activity of the Staff Common Room revolved. Such, naturally, as it was. For while Glenda Grower was the better-looking, Glenda struck rather than attracted; Penny was definitely pretty, and certainly the more approachable. And Penny was only twenty-three.

She was silently amused at the forms the approaches took: the clumsy grope from Bill Muggeridge; the galumphing puppyishness of Corbett Farraday; the appraising eye of Tom Tedder (for either loyalty to Miss Gilberd, or lethargy, prevented anything more tangible). About Toby, Hilary Frome was wrong. Appreciative though he was of Penny, ally though he felt her to be, there is between nineteen and twenty-three a great gulf fixed which prevented anything in the way of advances. Toby imagined Penny as a girl of infinitely greater experience and sophistication than himself, though, in looking back on her four years at Bedford College and her half year of unemployment thereafter, Penny could only be struck by the slim amount of worldly knowledge gained, the fleeting, unsatisfactory nature of the relationships formed. Thus, though she had little intention of responding more than politely to any of the advances, she enjoyed the game: it made her feel human. And that was not the feeling engendered by her relations with either of the Crumwallises, for example, or with Mr McWhirter.

As a rule the advances occurred either when she was alone with one or other teacher during a free period, or in the time between the end of school and the journey home. Most of the teachers lingered a few minutes in the staff room, not from any affection for the place, but to allow the unruly mob of boys to get down the long road that led to Cullbridge, and thence to disperse to the bus station, to Wimpy bars, the library or their various homes. Then the staff could walk home in peace. So though the place was as ill-furnished as it was ill-lit, they hung around there, putting books away in lockers, glancing at newspapers, knocking out their pipes or whipping through the odd bits of marking. Or, on occasion, making the odd concealed, subdued, terribly English pass at Penny.

'Ah well,' said Septimus Coffin, on the Monday after the Parents' Evening, 'it's four o'clock. The madding crowd seems to have ceased madding. At last the respectable citizen can take to the streets and get himself home.'

'I go the back way anyway,' said Bill Muggeridge, smelling as usual of stale sweat, and exuding a bullish discontent. 'No cause to rush home in my opinion.'

'Oh, I don't know,' said Coffin, tugging at his nicotine-stained moustache. 'As I get older I think more and more of my stomach, and I'm not ashamed to admit it. I'm promised a nice piece of rump steak with sauté potatoes. I'm beginning to smell them already.'

'You bachelors,' said Bill Muggeridge. 'All right for some.'

Septimus Coffin always resented that cheap jibe. In his young days unmarried men had been assumed to be wicked dogs, gay bachelors. Now they were assumed to be—well, gay, but not in the sense he acknowledged. And that he certainly was not. He merely grunted.

Mr Makepeace, who dreaded public places where he might meet the boys of Burleigh, sat longer than any, pretending to go through the disgracefully scrappy mathematics homework that his classes saw fit to throw his way. Toby, on the other hand, just looked in on the way to the boarding annexe, and popped straight out again, while Corbett Farraday had no particular fear of the boys—weren't they all boys together at Burleigh?—and stayed in the Staff Common Room for no other reason than to work himself up to an approach to Penny. He it was, that Monday, who plucked up courage to approach her, huffing and puffing around her with the slightly intimidating bonhomie of a young St Bernard.

'I say, *isn't* the weather fine,' he said, leaning over her and pushing his well-scrubbed face close to hers. He looked like an advertisement for baby-soap, grown up. 'I mean, it does look like being a *jolly* nice evening.'

'Yes, doesn't it?'

'Are you interested in wild flowers at all?'

Oh God, the approach botanic, thought Penny.

'Well, I haven't thought much, really, about . . . wild flowers.'

'Because the area round Cullbridge is awfully rich in rare species. I don't think many people know that.'

'No, I don't think they do.'

'It's a bit of a hobby of mine, actually. Sort of sideline. I wondered if one evening you'd like me to show you some of the things you can find . . .'

'Sort of nature ramble?' said Penny, gathering up her marking.

'That's the ticket. Awfully fun if you know what you're looking for. Then we could make for home, and you could meet Mother.'

Penny added to her load a pile of books she had in fact marked yesterday. Corbett Farraday's face fell, like a toddler whose jelly-baby has been snatched from its grasp.

'Oh, what a blow. Have you got all that marking tonight?'

' 'Fraid so, Corbett. Latin's not one of those languages you can teach with tape-recorders and acting little plays. You have to drum it into them. Some other night, eh?'

'Poor old Corbett,' said Septimus Coffin, as Penny shoved the books into her briefcase and made off down the drive. 'Never mind—none of the others have better luck.'

'Don't they?' said Corbett Farraday eagerly. 'Well, I suppose I'll have to keep trying. Mother's awfully anxious for me to bring a nice girl home. She's a Corbett, you know—that's who I'm named after. They used to be a big family in Cullbridge: milling and banking and that sort of thing. Mother says if I don't get a move on the line will die out.'

'Good Lord,' said Septimus Coffin. 'To think I may be looking at the last of the Corbetts.'

Glad she had avoided meeting Mrs Farraday (née Corbett), whom she imagined as some Gorgon straight from the pages of George Eliot, Penny swung down the drive, wishing she had not had to assume a double load of exercise books to avoid her. As she neared the front gates, Glenda Grower rode out from the path to the bicycle sheds and pedalled past her. A few yards on, though, she stopped, and turned her head round.

'You don't feel like coming round for a bite of supper tonight, I suppose?' she shouted.

Penny was conscious of the slightest of flushes coming to her face. To cover her confusion, something unusual with her, she said:

'I'd love to. Salisbury Cresent, isn't it?'

'That's it. Number five. About nine suit you?'

'Great.'

And with a wave Glenda Grower remounted, and rode stylishly through the gates. Penny strode on, regretting the flush that had risen to her cheeks, wondering if she had received her second tentative approach that afternoon.

One by one the teachers made their ways to their homes — modest, mostly celibate, mostly cheerless homes.

Corbett Farraday let himself into the moderately imposing Edwardian villa which he shared with his mother. He called a gay 'I'm back' in the direction of the lounge and started up the stairs. But he was halted by a massive 'Corbett!' and, putting a cheery face on it, he went towards the door behind which waited for him, looking indeed the spit image of Aunt Glegg in *The Mill on the Floss*, his mother.

Mr McWhirter had summoned a taxi to take him home, as he often did when afflicted with the snap and bite of chilblain pains. He had been first away, for he was not one to linger with colleagues. In the back of the taxi he snuffled contentedly at some (he thought) particularly witty riposte he had made to some piece of boyish impertinence from 3B in the final period of the day. Then he paid his fare, added a tip so meagre as to be barely decent, and shuffled across the pavement, through the front gate, and down the path to his semi-detached residence.

Whether or not there was a Mrs McWhirter was a matter of some debate at Burleigh. The general opinion was yes, but certain it was that no one had ever seen her. What could she be like? What kind of private life could be imagined for this dried-up bundle of chilblains and nasal catarrh? What Elaine waited in her tower for this shuffling Lancelot? The fact was, there was such a person, and there was even a daughter, now at Oxford. But Mrs McWhirter, cutting her losses, spent most of her time away, on the excuse that she was nursing her mother; and the daughter, if she felt like coming home, preferred to regard home as where her mother was. Mr

McWhirter did not regret them. He thought private life was a much over-rated thing. Once in the house, he carved himself a slice of meat from an ancient joint, put it on a slice of bread, and settled down at his desk with a sigh of pleasure, preparing to continue work on the Gaelic dictionary on historical principles which he had been occupied with now for nearly forty years.

There was never any doubt that Mr Makepeace lived alone. He had a ground-floor flat in a gloomy, yellow-brick, nineteenth-century house. He did not greatly mind the lack of light. At times he liked to sit there, with no more than two or three candles dotted about the room, imagining himself in some sort of shrine. Very frequently he was away from home, sampling the forms of service offered by the various high-church ecclesiastics in the area, driving determinedly over the countryside in a little red Mini that had become used to the eccentricities of his driving technique. Twice on Sundays he would thus venture forth, as well as to Evensong on Wednesdays and Fridays. And dotted through the year were the increasing number of Days dedicated to Saints who were honoured with his particular attentions. Such occasions, when he could worship the Saint in question on his or her (he had no sexual bias in these matters) day, in a church dedicated to him or her, in an atmosphere of tallow and incense, surrounded by flickering shadows and gorgeous vestments dimly perceived — these were the red-letter days of Mr Makepeace's life. And there was no chance whatsoever of meeting boys from Burleigh in a church.

Tonight he prepared, with an aesthete's excitement, his evening meal: he grilled a trout, prepared a butter sauce, boiled three potatoes of equal size, and a modest serving of fresh peas. Then he arranged the meal with mathematical precision on a plate, and took it to the dining table, placing it next to a dazzlingly white, freshly laundered napkin. He stood for a moment admiring it. It looked almost too good to eat. Then he fell to with relish.

Mr Makepeace, if the truth were known, was the most purely sensual of all the teachers at Burleigh School.

Monday evenings were always highspots in his week. For nearly six months now he had gone to Father Michael at St Cunegonde's for long, thrilling discussions about whether he had a vocation for the priesthood. Father Michael's personal opinion was that if Mr Makepeace had a vocation it was more for Drury Lane than for the Anglican Church. But he was a merciful man, and kept the conversations going, trying to probe if there was a grain of spiritual content implanted beneath Mr Makepeace's addiction to theatrical spectacle.

Dorothea Gilberd perched the tray on her mother's lap, and tucked the bedclothes fussily around her.

'It's haddock. I know you like haddock,' she said. 'Would you like the BBC News on?'

Mrs Gilberd, her mouth already full of food, grunted through her near-toothless gums, and spat food over her bed-jacket. Her daughter wiped her clean, and then went over to the little table and turned on the portable television.

'There we are. Don't suppose there'll be any good news, though, do you? Well, I'll go and have mine. I'll be back for the tray in two ticks.'

But she did not go back to the kitchen. Her mother's bedroom, once the living-room, was just off the hall, where the telephone was. The television sound had to be loud, though . . . Miss Gilberd picked up the receiver, and dialled.

'Tom?' she said, her voice low, giving to the conversation a touch of melodrama that Tom Tedder, at the other end, found distinctly ridiculous. 'Tom, I hate to bother you—you know I *do* try not to—but *could* I pop round tonight when I've got Mother settled? I'm upset—really upset . . .'

Tom Tedder's easy voice came reassuringly down the line. Dorothea Gilberd calmed down perceptibly.

'I expect I'm making a mountain—you know—but it was on my way home from school. Yes, today. And that beast Hilary Frome—I was in . . . But I'll tell you when I see you. About ten?'

She put down the receiver, feeling much happier, and even enjoyed the lukewarm haddock that was waiting for her in the kitchen.

'Do you have to change him in here, now?' demanded Bill Muggeridge, as he finished his evening meal of boiled mince and mashed potatoes.

'Piss off,' said Onyx unemotionally, pulling the disposable paper nappy on to the unappetizing baby with a remarkable lack of expertise, considering it was her fourth. 'It's got to be done.'

'I know it's got to be done. Looks as if it should have been done hours ago, if you ask me. I just asked whether it had to be done in here, while I'm eating.' He lifted his nose, like a gone-to-seed beagle. 'This place stinks like a French *pissoir*.'

He wasn't far wrong. Onyx notably lacked inclination for housework, not to mention motherly instinct. Which made it the more regrettable that, in an age when abortion is pressed on one as if it were a free sample, she should have contrived to have four children in six years—unwanted, dubiously parented, ill cared for. The previous one had never been clean before the next one arrived; they had had dummies shoved in their mouths to keep them quiet until they were four or five; and they crawled, ran and fell around the place—filthy, whining and hungry—until Onyx was forced to give them some of the attention they needed. Usually—it was a ploy—when her husband was eating.

'I didn't know you'd got so bleeding sensitive,' she said, pulling a filthy pair of leggings on over the nappy. 'Never used to be. This place doesn't smell any worse than the changing rooms at Colchester U's.'

'I didn't live in the changing rooms at Colchester U's. And that wasn't bloody babies. Christ, I'd like to see the end of bloody babies.'

'Just move out, any time you care to. Can't be too soon as far as I'm concerned. But don't forget to keep the cheques rolling in. Kids eat up the money.'

'Bloody hell,' said Bill Muggeridge, raging feebly. 'You can keep and feed your own bloody kids. Most of 'em aren't mine anyway.'

'As far as the law's concerned, they're all yours.'

Lacking Mr Bumble's power of repartee, Bill Muggeridge just muttered: 'That's a bloody laugh.'

'I don't know why you don't get old Crumwallis to make you head of the boarding section,' said Onyx, dumping the baby down in its playpen and ignoring its grizzles of discontent. 'Then you could move over there and we'd all be happy.'

'Oh yes—get shot of babies and land in the middle of a crowd of boys. I can't stand boys.'

'Oh, I don't know,' said Onyx.

That reminded Bill of something.

'Oh yes, and I saw you this afternoon.'

'Come again?'

'I saw you this afternoon. Walking over to the school.'

'So what? I was coming to have a yarn with Mrs Garfitt. She'd promised me a recipe.'

'That's a laugh, you and recipes. What were you going to do, set it to music? I suppose it was just by sheer chance you met up with Hilary Frome, was it?'

'Is that his name?'

'You know damned well what his name is. You talked

to him long enough.'

'I remember him from Parents' Evening. Pretty as a primrose, isn't he?'

'I saw you—putting on your little girl lost act. Brushing up against him.'

'Oh Gawd—sounds like something out of bleeding Barbara Cartland: "Suddenly she brushed up against him, and he knew that this was the real thing." Be your age. And if you want to know, I wouldn't have thought he was the type to be interested—not at all.'

'Hilary Frome would fuck the school cat if he thought he'd get a kick out of it.'

'Probably would at that. Well, I'll bear it in mind. I do sometimes fancy something a bit more refined.'

'Well, try a stick of barley sugar, for Christ's sake. If you go interfering with the boys we're out on our backsides.'

'Since you're moving out anyway, I don't see why you worry. I'd really try Crumwallis on this boarding lark.'

'Not a chance. He's got a head of the boarding section—salary nil per annum.'

'Oh yes, that nice little Toby Whatsit. Now, I'd say he had a really sensitive face, wouldn't you?'

Bill Muggeridge groaned.

'At least,' said Penny Warlock, 'you can say you *have* taught in a good school. As far as I'm concerned Burleigh is about the most dispiriting way possible to begin a teaching career. I'm beginning to think I'll leave in summer, whether I get a proper job or not. I'd plump for unemployment, given the choice.'

She sat back in the large, embracing armchair and took another mouthful of the splendid Spanish omelette. Glenda's cooking, like her everything else, was supremely competent. Penny made a mental note to get cold food from the delicatessen when she invited Glenda back.

'Of course, Burleigh is the dregs,' agreed Glenda, elegantly ingesting (rather than eating) the last scrap of food from her plate, and taking a goodly swig of white wine. 'But it has one enormous advantage over Bedfordshire Comprehensive.'

'Surprise me,' said Penny.

'It doesn't have girls.'

Penny, to her surprise, was surprised.

'I can see . . .' she tentatively began.

'I have had girls,' enunciated Glenda, 'up to *here*.'

'I don't suppose there's many girls that could be *that* much worse than, say, Hilary Frome,' put in Penny, out of loyalty to her sex.

'You think not? Oh, Hilary's a little charmer, I admit. Did I tell you what he did the other day, by the way? He'd been sitting apparently fascinated by my World Religions class, and when he came up at the end I made sure he wanted to ask a question about Zoroastrianism or Thuggee, or whatever damned thing I'd been going on about. Well, he smiled all ingratiatingly, then suddenly he asked if I wasn't tired of the Lesbian kick? He said he'd be happy to oblige me any time I"wanted it straight".Isn't that typically charming?'

'Good God. What did you say?'

'I said any time I wanted it straight I'd have it with someone who really enjoyed it straight. He switched on his sneer and took himself off.'

'My God, that boy . . .'

Glenda stood commandingly by the mantelpiece and took a cigarette.

'Nevertheless, anyone can take Hilary Frome's measure. We all have, apart from the Crumwallises, who carry moral and physical imperceptiveness to undreamed-of heights. On the other hand, my little charmer . . .'

'Your . . . ?'

'The one who put me in. Betty Maitland. My Betty,

star pupil of the arts line at Bedfordshire Comprehensive. Such a *sweet* girl. Everybody said so. And such an unblemished record. So that, when she went to the headmistress with what I was supposed to have done to her as we were changing after a singles tennis game, of course everyone believed her. Why would sweet Betty lie? Not a single one of my colleagues doubted for a moment what she said. The solidarity of women!'

'And there wasn't an atom of truth in it?'

'Not a scrap. I'd got fed up with her everlasting sweetness and shown her up in class the day before. Who would believe a sweet child would take that sort of revenge?'

'Wasn't there even a suspicion of truth in it? I mean, didn't you feel . . . perhaps . . . you would like to?'

'Oh, for God's sake,' said Glenda, throwing her cigarette disgustedly into the grate. 'You're just like the rest. Look, once and for all: I prefer men. I don't go for women, and I never have.'

Penny was conscious of feeling a twinge of disappointment.

Tom Tedder's flat was comfortable and untidy, like himself. Like him, too, it was daubed with paint. Specifically, several of his pictures hung on the walls, and one stood on an easel in the centre of the living-room. One and all testified to a staggering lack of talent. He had some of the techniques but none of the instincts of a painter. When he deprecatingly called them his 'daubs', nobody contradicted him. They depressed even him, though they comforted Dorothea Gilberd, who saw their value, and knew that Tom Tedder would never disappear to Chelsea, Arles, Florence or the South Seas.

Empty plates with crumbs from a chicken pie littered the floor around them as they sat in the late evening peace, that Monday night. Tom sprawled in the armchair, in an open, smock-like shirt, smoking. Dorothea sat at his feet, her head in his lap. If the spectacle of a woman well into her fifties in love with a man twelve years her junior is ridiculous, then they were ridiculous. Onyx Muggeridge would certainly, in her language, have had hysterics. But perhaps to more sympathetic eyes they were more touching than risible, and no more grotesque than many other lovers in whose relationship one loves overwhelmingly, and the other lets himself be loved, for whatever reason — convenience, self-importance, pity. Tom Tedder stroked Dorothea Gilberd's hair.

'That was good,' he said.

'Yes,' she agreed. Adding in her honest way: 'I didn't make it.'

'Feeling better now?'

'Oh *yes*. Much. You don't know.'

'Want to talk about it?'

Dorothea Gilberd thought. Thought back to the afternoon, as she stood in the delicatessen, that valued resort of the hard-pressed teacher bent on entertaining. Remembered Hilary Frome and Peter Quigly marching round the shelves singing 'Little Tommy Tedder, Sang for his supper'. Remembered the horrible, fair, insinuating Frome sidling up to her at the counter and suddenly, unexpectedly, braying out for the whole shop to hear in exaggerated cockney: 'Better not fatten him up too much, love, or he'll be too heavy to baby-snatch.' And the blush that rose, the helplessness, the looks of the other customers. No, she couldn't tell him, she just couldn't. And why spoil the perfection of this moment? Let it pass.

'Oh, I think I over-reacted,' she said. 'It wasn't much. Let's forget it.'

Tom Tedder grinned, behind her head. He thought: I bet she made it all up. He ruffled her hair affectionately.

*

On Monday afternoon and evening Toby once again enjoyed undisputed sway in the boarding annexe of Burleigh. Mr Crumwallis's brief eruption of activity was now again quiescent. Like all basically lazy people he was content to let things be not only when they were going well, but also when they merely appeared to be going well. The parents, he was convinced, had perceived nothing of the incident last Thursday, and therefore he was happy to relegate it to the back of his mind, and do nothing further about it.

After the usual bread and jam left out by Mrs Garfitt, Toby went and played a few games of rounders with the young boys. But his heart was not in it. He was turning over in his mind the best way to have a little talk with Pickerage.

He had been unable to prevent Pickerage going off on his own on Sunday. Sunday was the one day of the week when all the boys — particularly those of thirteen or over — enjoyed the largest possible freedom. It would have demanded from Toby a display of powers he was by no means sure he possessed to prevent Pickerage going off with Hilary Frome. Any appeal to the headmaster would have been quite useless, for at the mention of Hilary's name there would have snapped over his eyes those rose-tinted contact lenses he automatically assumed for viewing that young man. So he had adopted the feeble expedient of ringing the Frome household around tea-time, and asking to speak to Pickerage.

'Who?' Mrs Frome had asked. 'I'm afraid I don't know any boy of that name. Hilary's away for the day — gone on a long hike to tune himself up, as he put it. So sensible. I'm afraid I can't help you.'

'Sorry you've been troubled,' Toby had muttered, like a long-ago switchboard operator.

So presumably either Pickerage was lying about his date with Hilary Frome, or the pair had been up to something the whole of Sunday. Pickerage had gone straight to bed when he got back, and that day, Monday, had been something less than his dottily exuberant self. Toby was worried.

But it was far from easy to get to talk to him alone, at least without making a 'thing' of it, and that Toby was determined he would not do. Pickerage, with the cunning of adolescence, was finding expedients that kept him well out of Toby's way. He only appeared when the boys were half way through supper (corned-beef hash), and by then it was practically time for bed. Perhaps he could get him between breakfast and school.

'Time for bed for the younger ones,' he said at nine o'clock.

There was a general groan, but then they started upstairs, ragging and fighting and telling terrible jokes. Pickerage was in bed in two shakes—again unlike him— and apparently deep in a book under the sheets. Toby looked at him, and imperceptibly shook his head. He looked round at the rest of them. Young Tilney was cleaning his teeth with that concrete drill effect in the bathroom beyond the dormitory.

'You haven't washed your face, Wattling,' said Toby. 'Come on, hurry up—I know you haven't.'

With a groan Wattling got out of bed, and then danced cheekily into the bathroom. Toby saw him take up the pile of wet flannel from beside the bath and chuck it at his face. Then there was a piercing, terrified scream.

When he dashed into the bathroom Wattling's face was covered with blood, pouring from a gash that stretched from eye to chin. The palm of his right hand was oozingly red from another gash. Toby ran to the sobbing boy and took the flannel, and as he did so a naked razor blade fluttered down and tinkled on to the floor. The two of them looked at it, as blood dripped down on the cold linoleum.

CHAPTER 6

A CONCATENATION
OF CIRCUMSTANCES

It was typical of Edward Crumwallis that, even at this stage, his first reaction was an instinctive determination to cover up. It may be that he had missed his metier, and that he would have made a greater mark had he gone into politics.

'Ah—most unfortunate,' he said, standing in the blood-bespattered bathroom of the boarding section and looking at the pool on the floor as if it were a spilt cup of tea. 'But *not* very deep cuts. Now, perhaps if Mrs Crumwallis were to put some iodine on . . .'

'No!' howled Wattling.

'No,' said Toby, very firmly. Mrs Crumwallis's medical ministrations were so notorious for their vagaries that even Toby, a healthy young man with no great tolerance of the sick, would not willingly subject a boy to them.

'Well, perhaps just a bandage,' said the headmaster.

'No,' said Toby again, his heart in his mouth. 'The boy needs a doctor.'

'Mr Freely,' whinnied the headmaster, 'I think you—'

'It would be criminal not to get him proper attention. If that cut isn't seen to by somebody qualified the boy could be scarred for life.'

'Oh, nonsense. Fiddlesticks. Nothing but a surface cut. Naturally the cheek bleeds a little.'

'Do you think his parents are going to be happy when he comes home for the holidays with a scar the length of his face?'

Mr Crumwallis perceptibly weakened, and cleared his throat.

'They're going to ask what medical attention he had.'

'Mr Freely, I think you are usurping . . . er . . . I think you can rely on me to know . . . er . . .'

'Headmaster, I'm grateful to you for giving me almost sole charge of the boarders. I'm proud of your trust. But I feel I'm responsible for these boys now, and I feel I've failed them. If you don't phone for a doctor, I'm leaving Burleigh tomorrow.'

Mr Crumwallis gazed at him in amazement, as if the worm had turned, and left him flabbergasted at the depths of human ingratitude suddenly exposed. Then he caved in, and pottered off, muttering to himself, to telephone the school doctor.

Toby, next morning, was inclined to regard it as a great victory. It wasn't bad, he said to himself, at the age of nineteen, to be able to carry your point like that, especially when your antagonist was the headmaster, and you were an unpaid temporary assistant. In this appraisal of the situation Toby deceived himself. There is nobody in a stronger position than someone who is doing a good job of work for nothing, especially when his employer is stingy and congenitally idle.

Mr Crumwallis was very insistent that 'none of this should get out'. It was 'just an unfortunate accident,' he said. 'One of the senior boys being criminally careless.'

And certainly Broughton and one or two of the older boarders regularly drew a cheap safety razor over the blonde fuzz on their cheeks, and anxiously inspected the shavings as if they were virility tokens. Toby held his peace. He had won a victory, the doctor had come and put Wattling together again, and perhaps—though he didn't expect it—everything might return to normal.

Except, of course, that it was quite impossible that 'none of this should get out'. Next day it was all over the school. Ghoulish tales were told, by the boarders in every class, of the hideous pools of blood on the bathroom floor, of Wattling's terrified and ghastly aspect. In the very first hour one of Dorothea Gilberd's little boys had told her, and naturally at lunch break in the Staff Common Room she told everybody else. By the time Toby came in it was clear that the whole school knew. There was no point in holding anything back, so he didn't.

'According to the headmaster, it was just one of the older boys being careless with a used blade,' he concluded.

'Hmm,' said Septimus Coffin. 'What do you think?'

'The older boys hardly ever have used blades. One lasts them a term at least. And this one wasn't old. I picked it up off the floor, and it looked perfectly new.'

'Was it lying on top of Wattling's flannel?'

'No—as far as I can make out it was hidden in it. It must have been. Wattling always leaves his flannel lying in a heap by the bath. If the razor was on top of the heap, he would have been cut as soon as he touched it. My guess is that it was concealed inside.'

'Nasty,' shivered Dorothea Gilberd. 'Really malignant.'

'Taken with the other thing, you begin to wonder,' said Corbett Farraday. 'Has someone got a down on the school?'

'Or is it a maniac with a hatred of boys?' suggested Tom Tedder.

'He doesn't have to be a maniac to hate boys,' grunted Bill Muggeridge.

'But they're not weally the same, are they?' put in Mr Makepeace diffidently. 'I mean, the first was just a silly twick, a boy's pwank.'

'You mightn't have thought so if you'd seen them the next day,' said Toby.

'But you wouldn't think of that, the hangovers and all that, when you laced the fwuit cup, would you? But this is diffewent — weally vicious.'

'Well,' sniffled Mr McWhirter, with apparent relish, 'much more of this sort of thing and Crumwallis is going to start losing pupils.'

'Which would be good for none of us,' said Tom Tedder.

The odd thing was, that didn't seem to be how it struck McWhirter.

In the kitchens Mrs Crumwallis and the school cook were having one of their comfortable morning confabulations.

'And I said to 'im, I said: "All right, Mr Hodge, all right. There are other butchers in this town. Them neck-chops we 'ad last Friday was all fat an' gristle. They was rubbish, *and* they was full price. We don't mind you giving us rubbish, provided you charges us for it *as* rubbish." Now, was I right, Mrs C?'

Mrs Garfitt, fat, voluble and slovenly, paused for breath and gave a perfunctory stir to something that looked like workhouse broth on one of the meatless days.

'Quite right, Mrs Garfitt. A bit of fat never did a boy any harm, but we're not going to pay for it as if it was lean. We're not made of money.'

'I know that, Mrs C. Got to look to every penny. Got these at the baker's for next to nothin', by the by.' She drew from an enormous hold-all an array of archæological cakes and buns, and displayed them with pride. 'Might put 'em in the oven, freshen 'em up a bit.'

'That's a good idea, Mrs Garfitt. Is there a fairly good one there? We've got a boy in the sick bay.'

Mrs Garfitt picked up a cream horn and sniffed at it warily.

'Smells all right. Who is it? Hasn't got tummy trouble, has he?'

'No, no. It's Wattling. He had an accident with a razor blade.'

'Cor! Cheeky young blighter! All of thirteen and 'e's shaving 'isself. Makes you laugh, dunnit?'

Mrs Crumwallis's thought had apparently glided elsewhere, for she did not correct Mrs Garfitt.

'Now, lunch today is fish-cakes, and there's sausages tomorrow, Cornish pasty Thursday and shepherd's on Friday. Is that right?'

'Right. And that Hodge promised me some good cheap mince for the shepherd's. I'll make it tomorrow and shove it in the freezer.' She gave a final stir to the enormous pot. 'There. That's done. Though I says it as shouldn't, I could almost fancy a bowl o' that meself.'

It was next day, Wednesday, that Bill Muggeridge went to Mr Crumwallis and said he would be unable to take the Burleigh team to the All-Swessex Schools Swimming Championships on Thursday.

'Oh—ah—that's—er—most unfortunate. May I ask—er—why?'

Bill had expected that question, but he could not prevent there coming across his inward eye the memory of the grubby calendar in Onyx's kitchen, with the new red ring round Thursday the twenty-ninth.

'Family reasons,' he pronounced laconically.

Now family reasons can be anything from baby's colic to a wife running off with the milkman, and there is no arguing with them, because it is indelicate to inquire further, and potentially embarrassing to boot.

Mr Crumwallis blinked.

'Ah—yes—er—I see.'

It was a nuisance. Of course they could cancel Burleigh's participation. Not having a swimming pool, the boys merely had occasional periods at the Town Baths, and were unlikely to make any great splash in the swimming championships. On the other hand, they did have Willis, whose father was keen on swimming, and influential, and who had a fair chance in the 100 yards freestyle. No—it would look bad to cancel.

'Now what shall I do?' said Mr Crumwallis aloud. His first thought was to send Hilary Frome in charge. But then he remembered he had so far made little public display of his temporary teacher from Portlington. A public schoolboy, no less.

'I'll send young Freely with them,' he said.

Toby, when he was sent for, was perfectly willing.

'I don't know much about swimming,' he said, 'but I suppose it's mainly supervision, and getting the boys to the right races.'

'Quite,' said Mr Crumwallis. 'Quite. Mainly supervision.'

'What about the boarders?'

Mr Crumwallis drew himself up.

'I, of course . . . Oh, no. Goodness me, no. My wife and I have to go to the Cullbridge Athenæum's wine and cheese party. We are promised. Ah—I have it. I'll ask Hilary Frome to step in and see to things.'

'Hilary Frome?'

'Yes. Perfectly capable. And always willing to oblige.'

Toby opened his mouth. It was at this point, if any, that he would have to protest. But the fact that he had won a signal victory over the headmaster on Monday night made him reluctant to pit himself against him again so soon. The headmaster (Toby had some of the instincts of the minor public schoolboy) was, after all, the head. It was his school. What was more, it was in the highest degree unlikely that any protest of his would have the slightest effect in any matter relating to Hilary Frome. It was while he was dithering that the headmaster said:

'That will be all, Freely.'

And that was that. When Toby had gone, the headmaster got on to the organizer of the Championships.

'I'm afraid our regular chap has had to cry off. Trouble

at home, you know. But I'll be sending the boys with Freely, one of my temporary people. Tip-top young fellow, filling in time before Cambridge. Public schoolboy, you know . . . First class . . . Extremely responsible.'

And so it was settled. When Hilary Frome was approached he was, as the headmaster expected, perfectly amenable.

'Yes, that will be OK, Mr Crumwallis. Yes, I did have something on, but nothing I can't cancel. I'd like to do it. I've been a boarder, so I know the routine. Just you and Mrs Crumwallis go out and enjoy yourselves. Everything will be perfectly all right.'

That, then, was the concatenation of circumstances that lay behind the events of Thursday night: Bill Muggeridge noticing the ring on the kitchen calendar; Toby winning a victory over the headmaster on Monday night which made him chary of challenging him again on Wednesday; Mr Crumwallis deciding that, on balance, a public schoolboy who was on the staff would do more for the school's prestige than a young local, however personable. All these things, and other trifles light as air, took their place in the murder investigation that was to begin at Burleigh School on Thursday night.

CHAPTER 7

YOUNG MAN, I THINK YOU'RE DYING

Naturally, being worried, Toby chewed over the subject on Thursday before school with Penny Warlock. Equally naturally, by lunch break everybody was talking about it.

'The headmaster,' pronounced Mr McWhirter, 'has an almost total inability to judge the character of boys.' He emitted one of his painful-sounding nasal chuckles. 'But then, I have never in my life known a single headmaster of whom that might not be said.'

'Are you worried generally,' Septimus Coffin asked Toby, 'or is there something special?'

'Well, it's particularly Pickerage, I suppose. He seems to have elevated Hilary Frome into a sort of hero.'

'Not unusual.'

'No. But what I don't like is that Hilary Frome seems to spend a lot of time with him.'

'That is unusual. Schoolboy heroes usually keep their worshippers at a distance.'

'Yes. But they seem to have spent the day together on Sunday. Pickerage said Frome was going to teach him to play squash, and then take him home to introduce him to his parents. That would be strange enough, but the fact is, he didn't.'

'I'm not surprised at that,' said Coffin. 'What sixteen-year-old is going to take a thirteen-year-old home to meet his oldies? Parents are not that slow on the uptake, and his father is a doctor.'

'Still,' said Toby, 'I'd like to know what they did do. And Pickerage has been very reserved since — quite damped down.'

'Pickerage,' contributed Tom Tedder, 'is rather out of commission at the moment. He was looking very hot and flushed in woodwork just now, and I sent him along to Mrs C. She took his temperature — about the only thing she *can* do — and sent him to bed.'

'Oh,' said Toby, with an expression of puzzlement. 'I wonder if that makes it better, or worse.'

'I think you're worrying needlessly,' said Dorothea Gilberd comfortably. 'I mean, what can he actually *do*?'

Nobody cared to enlighten her, and after an embarrassed silence the conversation turned to other matters.

*

The bus was to come to Burleigh for the swimmers at five-thirty, and then drive to Sturford, the county town, where the championships were to take place. Toby checked carefully through the boarding annexe after school, and then there was nothing to be done but hand over to Hilary Frome. This was done with the frigid politeness of two people who do not like each other, know they do not like each other, but have never let that dislike come out into the open. Little icicles like daggers hung in the atmosphere.

'Supper is in the kitchen,' said Toby, speaking to Hilary in the upstairs corridor of the boarding section. 'It's cold, so there's no problem. The younger boys go to bed at nine o'clock. I usually read to them a bit, but there's no need for you to. Just let them read in bed for ten minutes or so, and then put the lights out. Oh, and Pickerage is in the sick bay.'

'Oh, I know,' said Hilary Frome, with deliberate, impertinent provocation. 'Pickerage is a friend of mine.'

'Yes,' said Toby, and cleared his throat uneasily. 'Well—Mrs Crumwallis says he's to have another dose of—of medicine before he goes to sleep.'

The two of them looked towards the little wooden table outside the sick bay, where a bottle labelled 'Dr MacLaren's Stomach and Bowel Mixture' stood, together with a large spoon. The label on the bottle bore a picture of Dr MacLaren, who looked as if he might have been personal physician to Mr Gladstone. If the two had liked each other more, they might have cast their eyes heavenwards. As it was, they made no sign.

'Two tablespoons,' said Toby. Hilary Frome nodded coolly.

'Oh, and I don't know if you're going to play any games with the younger boys before it gets dark—'

It was out before Toby could stop it. Boy as he still was, he blushed.

'I might,' said Hilary Frome. 'Before it gets dark.'

'Well, I shouldn't let Wattling play,' continued Toby hurriedly. 'He's only just out of the sick bay himself, and he might fall over and open up that cut again.'

'Of course,' said Hilary. 'Poor old Wattling. Perhaps he can just sit around and score.'

'Yes. Well, I'd better be getting down to the bus . . . I expect I'll be back by eleven or so.'

'Right you are,' said Hilary, turning away as if terminating the interview. 'Cheer on Willis. From me.'

You cool little sod, thought Toby, and reluctantly went down to the front drive.

In the event, Hilary rummaged around in the gym and found a cricket bat and ball. The smaller boys could have some bowling and catching practice. Admittedly it was only March, but the cricket season could never come too early for Hilary. He knew he looked well in white flannel. He rounded them all up, and ushered them out on to the lawn.

'Just going for a bit of a hit, Malcolm,' he called, as they went past the sick bay. 'You won't be lonely?'

'No, Hilary,' came the muffled voice of Pickerage.

Hilary, of course, batted, and the boys took it in turn to bowl. The rest stood round the outskirts of the lawn, poised to catch. Wattling had tagged on, plastered up as he was, and Hilary included him in. He wasn't going to take orders from a jumped-up sixth-former. Hilary batted with style, in the manner of a latter-day Raffles, distributing possible catches around the lawn. He really looked very well indeed.

That, at any rate, was what the headmaster thought, watching him keenly from his sitting-room, sipping a cup of atrocious coffee. A real credit to the school, he thought. He meant, in fact, a real ornament, for Hilary Frome was ornamental rather than creditable, but the two things elided in his mind. The headmaster expanded into geniality as he contemplated his own cleverness in ensuring that Hilary Frome remained at Burleigh for his GCE year. Indeed, he regretted bitterly that his attempts to establish a sixth form in the school had been so abortive. Those boys (they were few, for academic impulses withered and died in the Burleigh air) who aimed at Advanced Level, or even university, had always trickled off into the state system as soon as they had taken their Ordinary Levels, if not before. A criminal waste. Imagine what Burleigh might achieve, Edward Crumwallis thought, with Hilary Frome as its head boy for two or three years!

Hilary Frome knew he was being watched. He always had a consciousness of that, as a beautiful woman does. When the light began to fail he despatched Tilney with the bat and ball to the gym, and sent the others ahead to the boarding annexe. Then he strolled, slowly and elegantly, in that direction himself.

'Ah, Frome . . . One moment.'

It was the headmaster, calling him from his sitting-room window. Somehow Hilary had known he would.

'Ah — Frome,' said Edward Crumwallis, as Hilary walked respectfully in. 'Splendid idea of yours, getting in a bit of advance practice for the season. Excellent notion. Any talent there, do you think? Well, time will show, eh? You seem to have an excellent way with them, with the younger ones. You have, if I may say so, the right touch.'

'Thank you, sir,' said Hilary demurely.

'You know, Frome, it gives me a great deal of pleasure to think of you as head boy here next year. A school, you know, is like — ' here the headmaster came to a halt, because he had launched into a metaphor without having a metaphor readily to hand; and in fact he had very few notions of what a school was like — 'is like the human body. Know what I mean?' Hilary Frome nodded intelligently. 'It may seem healthy enough, but it's no use if what's up here—' he tapped his head—'isn't up to scratch. It's what's up top that counts. It's like that with a school. We've got a fine little school here, I'm sure you'd agree—' Hilary Frome looked at him with a light of pure idealism in his eyes, but he drew the line at assenting—'but what's going to count in the years ahead is what we've got up top. And one of those things is you, Frome.'

Hilary swallowed, apparently with emotion.

'I'm sure I'll try to pull my weight, sir,' he said, his damask cheek giving no sign of the tongue inside it.

'I know you will, Frome. I've always known it. I may say without vanity that I'm rarely mistaken in a boy. And I can see that for the tasks that lie ahead of you in this school you are splendidly equipped. Quite splendidly equipped.'

Hilary Frome was afflicted by a cough.

'I can see already what a fine relationship you have with the other boys. Firm, yet friendly. Build on it, Frome. And there's one more thing I wanted to say.'

'Yes, Mr Crumwallis?'

'I appreciate your stepping in like this. Filling the breach, holding the fort, and that kind of thing. I may treat you as a grown-up person, may I not? Should you feel like a glass of—er—sherry in the course of the evening, by all means come and pour yourself one!'

He waved his hand munificently in the direction of the sideboard, as if it were the bar at White's. Hilary Frome glanced politely in its direction, and saw the two bottles of sherry left over from the last staff festivities, one of them half empty, the other two-thirds empty.

'Thank you very much, sir. If I feel like a glass, I certainly will have one.'

'Good,' said the headmaster. 'Good . . . And now Mrs Crumwallis and I must wend our way to the Athenæum. A fine organization, Frome. Father's a member, eh? One day I hope you will be.

His back was already turned, so he did not see Hilary Frome's gesture, expressive of what he could do with the Cullbridge Athenæum.

'Hello, Malcolm,' said Hilary Frome, pausing at the door of the sick bay on his way to the boarders' common room. 'How are you feeling?'

'Pretty rough,' said Pickerage, who certainly looked less than his usual perky self. 'I think I caught a cold on Sunday.'

'Did you now?' said Hilary, coming in to the sick bay, which was really no more than a scruffy little room with only a slight hospital smell about it to bespeak its function. 'One more thing for you to hold against me. Never mind, I'll be coming to give you your medicine later on.'

'Ugh. Mrs Crumwallis's muck.'

'Now, now. Remember I am the apple of the head-master's eye. His right hand . . . testicle.'

Pickerage giggled.

'He has just told me that if I continue in my present path, remain the fine, upstanding, clean-living boy I so evidently am, I may one day hope—wait for it—to be elected to—Gracious heavens!—the Cullbridge Athenæum!'

'Big deal!' cried Pickerage, regaining something of his usual Senate page-boy look. Hilary seemed to have got the reaction he wanted, and, looking pleased, he went over to the window.

'What are you looking at?'

'Surveying the stately grounds, enjoying the splendid view to be had from Burleigh's magnificent hospital facilities.' He peered into the gathering gloom. 'Well, well: you can see over to the sports field.'

'So what? We don't play floodlit football.'

'Even to the sports pavilion. Well, well.'

Suddenly he dashed over to the door and put out the light.

'What are you doing, Hilary?'

'Seeing, but not being seen . . . Ah, just as I thought . . . Poor old Muggeridge.'

'Muggeridge? What's he doing here at this time of night? Why didn't he go with the swimmers if he's not doing anything?'

'Wouldn't you like to know! There are parts of my life, my dear Malcolm, that even you are not privy to. Elements in my grand strategy that, as commander, I do not care to confide in you . . . Cowardly timorous beastie as you are . . . Whoops! He's tripped over a root . . . There he goes, off into the trees.'

He glanced round in the darkened room.

'Well, Malcolm, what are we going to do with you?'

'Switch on the light, Hilary. I don't like the dark.'

'Baby . . . There you are . . . Well, now I'm in charge of this great boarding establishment, how are we going to amuse ourselves?'

Pickerage, already flushed, looked down at the sheets, hot and bothered.

'I don't know . . .'

'Come on, shy little miss. What's up?'

'Well, I don't want to do . . . what we did on Sunday.'

'You don't want to do what we did on Sunday, do you not, you prim little Victorian? And why, pray, not?'

'I didn't like it . . . It was nasty . . . It hurt.'

'Really? What a shame. It didn't hurt me. It'll be easier next time. We make a great partnership, Malcolm.'

'Don't start on about *that* again. I don't want to.'

'Who's starting on about anything? . . . You wouldn't like me to adopt someone else as my protégé, would you, Malcolm?'

'Oh *no*, Hilary!'

'Well, then, we *are* going to make a partnership, aren't we?'

Hilary Frome sat down on the bed.

'And if it hurt you, that's not the only fun there is, is it? You prefer the old kind, do you? Conservative little thing. But the old kind is a very good kind.' He slid his hand down under the sheet. 'Awfully nice . . . warming . . . satisfying . . . Isn't it, Malcolm?'

The ancient television in the boarders' common room was giving a reasonable picture for a change. ITV had a good traditional Western on, in which the grizzled old sheriff (played by a clapped-out Hollywood actor who had kept out of politics) taught the rules of the game and his homespun philosophy to his tearaway young deputy (played by a reformed pop star). It was just the sort of thing the boys liked, and when Hilary had fetched their suppers—a cold Scotch egg each—from the kitchen, they all sat watching it. The younger boys did not take at all kindly to Hilary lounging in a superior way in front of the set and drawling out the dialogue before it got spoken.

'Sometimes a man's gotta do . . .'

'Oh, shut up, Hilary! You're spoiling it.'

'Womenfolk's just like cattle, boy. You treat 'em rough but you treat 'em fair.'

'Put a sock in it, Frome.'

The film drew towards its close, the inevitable shoot-out round the hanging rock.

'Well—bed for the teeny-weenies.'

'Oh, get stuffed, Hilary. We're going to watch to the end.'

Recognizing the limits of his power, Hilary gave in ungracefully.

'Well, well—to think there are people in this world who can't guess how *that* will end. So be it. I hope you realize you could get me into trouble with the Great God Crumwallis. If it's not over in ten minutes—bed all the same.'

But ten minutes sufficed for the blazing gun-fight, and for the affecting death scene with soaring strings. Then Hilary kicked the boys along to the dormitory, and supervised their minimal ablutions.

'Kindly inspect your flannel, Wattling, in case your hidden enemy has concealed a Samurai sword in it . . . Do shut up, Tilney: no wonder little Toby is such an insensitive oaf, if he has to listen to that racket every night . . . Is that tear in your pyjamas due to the age of the garment, Martins, or is it a feeble attempt to be provocative?'

Finally he got them all into bed.

'Right. Ten minutes' reading, then lights out.'

'Aren't you going to read to us?'

'I am *not*. You're confusing me with Nanny Freely. You'll have to wait to see what happens to the Famous Five until he can read it to you in his own inept fashion. I have to go and see Pickerage.'

There was a satirical moan.

'Enough of your jealousy. I'm only going to give him his medicine.'

There was another satirical moan. Hilary marched off coolly, and continued along the corridor.

'Right,' he said at the door of the sick room. 'And how do we feel after the Frome treatment?'

'Not bad,' said Pickerage, looking perky. 'All right, really.'

'Good. And now the patient must have the Crumwallis treatment.'

'Oh, come on, Hilary. I feel better. Honestly. Anyway, that stuff is stomach medicine. Mrs C.'s got no idea. There's nothing wrong with my stomach.'

'Nevertheless, swallow it down you must. Two table-spoonsful, as prescribed by Florence Nightingale Crumwallis, the lady with the lamp and the face like a granite quarry.'

Pickerage laughed in spite of himself. Hilary Frome fetched the bottle and spoon from the corridor, and took a glass from the cabinet by the window.

'Oh, come on, Hilary. Pour it down the sink.'

Hilary was distracted by the window, and peered out into the darkness, watching for signs of movement.

'All quiet on the Western front . . . No, medicine it is, I'm afraid, Malcolm, old boy. I cannot betray my ter-rust. I'll tell you what I'll do, though. Old Crumwallis said I could have a glass of sherry. Think of that! A . . . glass . . . of . . . sherry! From the headmaster's own cellar! What princely munificence! Well, I'll go and get myself a glass, and we'll drink together.'

'I don't see how that benefits me. I've still got to drink that ukky medicine.'

'Ungrateful little swine,' said Hilary. 'I'm promising you a gracious occasion, so try to behave with a bit of *savoir faire*. If you're good I'll let you have a sip or two of the head's genuine Cyprus Amontillado, to wash down Dr MacLaren's bowel mixture. We haven't had a chance of drinking together, have we, Malcolm? Due to the lunacy of the English licensing laws. Perhaps next summer we could go to the Continent—drink at a pavement café. I'll go get me that sherry.'

At the door Hilary bellowed along the corridor to the junior dormitory:

'Lights out!'

Then he darted downstairs. When he returned two or three minutes later, he brought with him the fragrance (in Dickensian phrase) of a fairy emerging from a wine vault, and hiccoughing.

'You've had one already,' said Pickerage.

'A mere soupçon. Old Crumwallis won't notice I've had more than his miserly allowance. He doesn't care for drink, or for any of the good things of life. And anyhow, I'm his blue-eyed boy. He wouldn't begrudge me an extra glass. Now . . . two tablespoonsful, Nurse Toby said.'

'Ugh. That stuff's disgusting. Can't we throw it away, Hilary? Look at the bottle. It's about a hundred years old. You're not supposed to keep medicine that long.'

'Nonsense. They just never change the label. Mrs Crumwallis uses gallons of the stuff. Probably keeps the firm in business. This came fresh last week from their labs in Birmingham — just by the detergents factory . . . Right, now here's your glass . . . Now, let's drink.'

There was a bang, and a flutter of suppressed laughter from along the corridor. Hilary went to the door and shouted.

'Quiet there, you infant menaces, or I'll be along and slipper the lot of you in a minute.'

Then he came back.

'Right, Malcolm, let's have a toast. I propose — sounds a bit corny, but toasts always do — I propose "To Us". Come on — bottoms up, luvvy.'

He grinned a charming smile as he assumed the cockney charwoman's accent, and they both raised their glasses and drank.

Ten minutes later, Mr and Mrs Crumwallis, returning earlier than they expected from the wine and cheese do, heard even from their quarters the noise from the boarding section. Running to the connecting door they opened it, and stared aghast at the scene.

Hilary Frome, stretched face down along the floor, was writhing and retching at the top of the stairs. Around him, wide-eyed, curious, afraid, were the boarders, young and old. Broughton, the oldest boarder, was slapping Hilary on the back, then in desperation pushing him over and trying to massage his stomach.

'Get it up, whatever it was, Hilary. For Christ's sake get it up. Tilney, for pity's sake go and call a doctor. I don't understand what to do. Get on the phone to his dad, for Christ's sake!'

But it was the head who ran to his study to phone. And it was Mrs Crumwallis who ran up the stairs and incompetently took charge. And it was leaning his head on Mrs Crumwallis's bosom that, ten minutes later, Hilary Frome expired. Connoisseur of bizarre sensations though he was, it was probably not the deathbed Hilary would have chosen.

CHAPTER 8

MR CRUMWALLIS'S CONSTERNATION

Within an hour of Mr Crumwallis's telephone call to the school doctor, the police were in residence at Burleigh. Within an hour and a half a detective-superintendent had arrived from Sturford, and had taken charge.

Somebody had to. Mr Crumwallis, the fragile façade of his public personality shattered, seemed to be in a state of near-breakdown. He shouted directions to the boarders, and, when they were ignored, he shouted contrary orders. He and Broughton carried the dead body of Hilary Frome from its resting place at the top of the stairs, and laid it on the bed in the sick bay. The doctor, when he arrived, tut-tutted at this, but he decided that this — like everything else — was a matter for the police. When Superintendent Pumfrey arrived, charging in like a drill sergeant-major bursting in on some particularly slack recruits, he found the local Cullbridge Police already well into the routine work, with the Crumwallises fussing around upstairs and downstairs, vocal but ineffectual. A little knot of boys, white but wide-eyed, stood in the doorway of the dormitory. From inside Pumfrey could hear the sound of a boy crying.

'By gum!' he expostulated, more to himself than to his sergeant or anybody else. Then he raised his voice in the direction of the only civilian male adult around.

'Are you a master here?' he demanded.

Mr Crumwallis let out a high whinny.

'Er— *headm*—'

'Well, please go to your quarters. Or somewhere away from these stairs. Enough seems to have been destroyed already. The photographers will have to make what they can of what's left. I shall need a room—'

'There are—er—classrooms . . .'

'Do you have a study?'

'Er—yes.'

'That will do.'

Mr Crumwallis, even in his broken state, muttered aggrievedly to himself that the Superintendent hadn't *asked*, and Mrs Crumwallis stared at Pumfrey with stony dislike. The head pointed, offendedly, in the direction of his own quarters.

'Through there.'

'Right. Will you please hold yourselves ready. But keep away from the stairs and the sick bay . . . Oh glory, what's that?'

That was the door of the boarding annexe banging open, and Toby Freely and four of the boarders dashing in.

'What's happened? Why are all those—?'

'Who are you?' bellowed Pumfrey, in his most parade-ground voice. 'Head boy or something?'

'Er— Mr Freely,' murmured the headmaster. 'In charge of the boarding section. Er— a *Portlington* boy.'

Superintendent Pumfrey looked at him in bewilderment, then turned back to Toby.

'Right. You look competent enough. Get all those boys

into the dormitory, and keep them there. I don't care what you do—I don't suppose the little blighters will go off to sleep—but keep them there and out of the way of my men—right? And be *careful* when you go up the stairs—OK?'

'There's a fire-escape we could use.'

'Right. Use it. Though it's a bit like shutting the stable door. Now—where's this study?'

And with Superintendent Pumfrey marching off through the door into the private quarters of the Crumwallises, the investigation into the death of Hilary Frome began in earnest.

Superintendent Michael Pumfrey came from the Swessex Police Headquarters at Sturford. Swessex, a bastard county created by the iniquitous reorganization of local government in the early 'seventies, comprised one and a half old counties knocked together because it looked neater that way. It was therefore larger than the old units, and infinitely more inefficient. Sturford, however, was no more than twenty miles away from Cullbridge, so Pumfrey's take-over at the scene of the murder had been reasonably quickly achieved. Michael Pumfrey had spent part of his childhood in Cullbridge, though the existence of Burleigh School had made no particular impression on him at the time. When he had been shown the study he drew in Sergeant Fenniway, pointedly shut the door, and said again 'By gum!'

He was not, in fact, from the North Country, but he knew no better expression for letting off steam and easing pent-up irritation. He held his temper on a pretty short fuse, and it was as liable to explode in the face of a headmaster as in that of a dustman. More liable. He was not tall, close to minimum height in fact, but he was stocky, and he made up for lack of inches with a pressing, high-speed manner which sometimes made people think he was all noise and movement and no intelligence. In fact, the noise and movement were outward expressions of a relentlessly ticking brain. His hair was slicked back in a manner popular in the 'fifties, and his hardbitten face was hardly softened by a neat black moustache of the sort that Herr Hitler had driven out of fashion.

Once in the room he looked again at Fenniway and let out a splutter of irritation.

'That's someone I'm going to bite the head off of before this investigation's over!'

'Not his usual self at all,' said Fenniway. 'Came here myself as a boy once—playing football. Very different he was then. Condescending as you like. The lord of the educational manor condescending to fraternize with the plebs.'

'Is that so? Doesn't surprise me. It seems he goes to pieces in a crisis, then. Not what one expects from a headmaster. Did I gather he had only just arrived back?'

'Apparently. The boy—his name's Hilary Frome, by the way—was retching at the top of the stairs when he and that hatchet-faced wife of his got in. I talked to the boy who'd been trying to help this Frome—trying to get him to vomit it up, and so on. It was no use, he said. The headmaster couldn't have done anything.'

'That's as maybe. I'd like to know exactly why he's gone so completely off his head. There's a local doctor called Frome. Could be a pretty influential parent. Should we speak to this Crumwallis first, do you think, while the technical chaps are playing their games upstairs?'

'Well,' said Fenniway, 'I gather there's a boy—'

'Oh?'

'A young lad. He was in the sick bay.'

'I saw some damnfool medicine up there.'

'Yes. It was for him. I gather Frome was in the room with him when he—well, started retching.'

'Hmmm. Best see him and get it over. Then he can go

to bed if he's nothing to do with it. Not that the poor chap's likely to get much sleep tonight.'

Superintendent Pumfrey looked around the study, and once more said, 'By gum!'

'Something getting you, sir?'

'I don't know . . . Pretty rum kind of school this, wouldn't you say, Fenniway? Would you send your son here?'

'He's about minus three months at the moment, sir, if that's what it is.'

'Oh well, I don't think this is the kind of place you have to put them down for at birth. Plenty of time for you to make a decision. I don't know what it is about this study . . . sort of phoney. These books — they look like a second-hand bookshop.'

'Probably does buy books at that kind of place.'

'Yes. But it looks as if he went in and said "I'll have that wall." To furnish the study.' Mike Pumfrey punched the books aggressively, and then peered at them. 'Look, here's Southey's *History of the Peninsular War* next to *Angel Pavement*. And here's volume one of *Old Mortality* with volume two over there. Just shoved up on the shelves with no order or reason. Like . . . like a stage set. What was that play all the amateur dramatics people used to do?'

'Amateur dramatics was a bit before my time, sir.'

'Nonsense. They're still at it. You just plonk your arse down in front of the telly and don't realize. What was that play? *The Happiest Days of Your Life*. That's it. This looks like a set for *The Happiest Days of Your Life*.' A thought struck him. 'Well, I don't think those kids up there are going to count this as one of them.'

He turned back to Fenniway. 'I'm wasting time. Will you get that kid in?'

Fenniway crossed through again into the boarding annexe, and sent a message up by one of the constables helping the technicians on the stairs. After a wait Toby came along the upstairs corridor and sent Pickerage down with an encouraging pat on the shoulder. Pickerage looked as if he needed it.

'Everything all right?' Fenniway called up to Toby. Toby looked down and grimaced.

'As well as can be expected, as they say.'

Which was about how you would describe Pickerage. He had clearly been sobbing fit to burst, but he was now past that. His face, however, was smeared by the dabbings he had made at it with a stupendously dirty handkerchief. He was conspicuously trying to be brave, but it was quite clear he had been devastated by the experience. Even now, quiet, there seemed to be a sob perpetually at the back of his throat. One thing about him struck Pumfrey as being unboyish: he seemed to be taking no pleasure from being so sensationally at the centre of things.

Mike Pumfrey had wondered whether the two of them might sit and talk things over in the two easy chairs—stained, dusty, pre-war relics, that squatted capaciously in the far corner of the study. But he thought something more normal might pay dividends, something that was more within the boy's everyday range of experience, so he sat himself behind the headmaster's desk and cultivated an air of briskness. As soon as he saw Pickerage he knew he had been right: here was a boy who had often gone for interviews in the headmaster's study.

'Right, now, sit down, old chap. I realize this has been a horrible thing to happen to you. But we're going to talk to you first, and then you can start putting it behind you. We've got to find out exactly what happened before this boy—Hilary Frome, is that the name?—died, and you're the one who can help us.'

Pickerage nodded dully.

'Now, what exactly happened?'

'When Hilary died, you mean?'

'Then and earlier. Let's go back a bit, shall we? You were in the sick bay, weren't you?'

'Yes. I had a fever. I think I caught a cold on . . . on Sunday.' Pickerage gulped. 'Anyway, Hilary came in—'

'Hold your horses. Was Hilary a boarder?'

'Oh no. He was in charge because Toby had to go with the swimmers to Sturford. Hilary's going to . . .' He stopped. 'He was going to be head boy next year. He was my friend.'

'I see. That's why you're so upset, is it?' Pickerage paused, and then nodded. Perhaps he felt there was no point in pretending not to be upset. 'So you were in the sick bay, and naturally Hilary came to see you. When was that?'

'He shouted to me as he was going out to play cricket with the other boys. Then, when they came in, he came up to see me for a bit.'

Pumfrey noticed that a slight flush came into Pickerage's face, and he looked down at his hands, clasping and unclasping themselves nervously in his lap.

'And what did you talk about? What did you do?'

Pickerage said hurriedly; 'We talked about Muggeridge. Hilary went to the window and looked out, and he said Muggeridge was stalking around outside.'

'I see. Is that the caretaker?'

'Oh no.' Pickerage, wide-eyed and somewhat scornful, was clearly incredulous that anybody should not be familiar with the details of his own small world. 'Muggeridge is the games master. He's awful. All smelly, and then he gets downs on you, and takes it out on you. He was supposed to go with the swimmers.'

Click-click went the little machine in Pumfrey's brain that was card-indexing all this information, putting arrows against all the possible trails. Normally he would have taken notes, but he knew that Pickerage would be doubly uneasy if he did that.

'I see,' he said. 'And then?'

'And then he went away and watched the television with the others. Later on I heard him go with them to the dorm. Then he came down to—' the boy gulped—'to give me my medicine.'

'That's the medicine we found in the sick bay, is it?'

Pumfrey had already noticed it was a patent stomach medicine. Pickerage nodded, and then, in a sudden access of indignation, said:

'That's right. Old mother . . . Mrs Crumwallis gives you just anything. It's not right. She's no idea. She could kill you.' He caught himself up in horrified confusion. 'Anyway, I said I didn't want to take it. There's nothing wrong with my stomach. We could have poured it down the sink. But Hilary said I had to. And he said he'd go down and get himself a sherry.'

'A sherry?'

'From the head's sitting-room. Oh—it was all right. Old . . . Mr Crumwallis had said earlier on that he might. So Hilary said.'

'So he was going to have a drink with you and help you get yours down, was that the idea?'

'Yes. Anyway, he was gone a few minutes, and he came back smelling—you know. My mum likes sherry, so I know the smell. Awful when she kisses you.'

'So he'd had one already.'

'Yes. But he said old Crumwallis would never notice. So then he got my medicine from outside—'

'Outside?'

'Yes. It was standing just outside in the corridor.' A trace of Pickerage's natural urchin grin wafted over his face. 'I suppose Mrs C. thought I'd be swilling it down like an alcoholic if she left it in the room. Anyway, Hilary brought it in, and put two tablespoonsful in a glass. Then we had a sort of toast . . .'

'Ah, yes. What was that?'

' "Good health," ' lied Pickerage. 'And then we drank. And then he rushed off to the bathroom and started throwing up.' His eyes filled with tears. 'It was horrible. And he came out into the corridor. I think he was trying to call for help. And Broughton came. And then all the others. And I went out, and Hilary was crying out, you know, and . . .'

Two enormous tears welled out of Pickerage's eyes and ran rapidly down his cheeks, followed by others. He looked down miserably, and then wiped them away.

'Well,' said Pumfrey briskly, 'we can hear about the rest of it from Broughton, can't we? That's all been very helpful. One little thing: where did Hilary get the glass for his sherry? From down here?'

'No. He took one from the cupboard in the sick bay. She doesn't leave medicines there, but she leaves a lot of dirty old glasses and bowls and thermometers and things. He could have got one from the kitchen, but I expect he'd locked up after he'd brought the supper up.'

'Ah—there'd been supper. Had you had any?'

'No. I didn't feel like it.'

'I see. Right, well, is there anything else you can think of?'

Pickerage sat huddled miserably in his chair. He swallowed hard once or twice. His face was drooping into his chest, but Pumfrey saw him half look up at him, then duck sharply down again. Finally he muttered:

'Hilary was my friend.'

'Yes . . .'

'I don't want to stay in this place now he's . . . dead.'

'Oh, come on. I'm sure you've got other friends. You may feel like that now . . .'

Suddenly Pickerage looked up and spoke very loudly.

'I don't want to stay in this school at all. I'm afraid. I want to go away. Go away somewhere else.' His voice was rising into hysteria, and suddenly he burst voluptuously into tears. 'I don't want to sleep in the dorm. Somebody might try to kill me. I'm afraid. I'm so . . . afraid.'

Then Pumfrey did try to comfort him, as he would have done one of his own. After a little Pickerage calmed down, but only with a palpable effort. Pumfrey took him upstairs and, after consultation with Toby, they put him to bed in Toby's room, and locked the door. He gulped a little, but the notion of locking the door certainly seemed to make him feel happier. As he went down again, and traversed the headmaster's hall on his way to the study, Pumfrey thought he caught a glimpse of the head's pallid face through the crack of an open door. He gave no sign of having seen.

'What did you make of him?' Pumfrey asked Fenniway.

'Lively kid. Lively normally, I mean. Horrible thing to happen when you're that age.'

'Yes . . . I think he was hiding something, you know. Or keeping something back.'

'Like what?'

Pumfrey shrugged. 'Hard to guess. Could have been just nothing—some little schoolboy sin. Could have been vital.'

' "Hilary was my friend," ' quoted Fenniway. 'There may have been something there.'

'Quite likely. He blushed now and then. But I thought there was something else . . . I wouldn't want to have that woman treating one of my kids if he was sick, would you? . . . You notice how he said "I want to go somewhere else"? Not "home". Poor bloody kid . . . The boy upstairs seems to do a good job . . . It would be a pretty terrible place, this boarding section, if there was just the headmaster and his wife.'

Beautifully on cue, there was a knock at the door. Pumfrey lifted his eyebrows at Fenniway, and shouted: 'Come in.'

'I wondered,' said the voice of the headmaster, piping insecurely as he insinuated himself round the door, 'if Mrs Crumwallis could get you something. Tea? Coffee?'

'No,' said Pumfrey. '*No*.'

'Ah . . . I see you've talked to Pickerage,' said Mr Crumwallis, his long, bony body now fully inside and draped up against the doorpost, his head poked forward, the whole effect being to make him look like a bereaved ostrich. 'Poor little boy,' he went on, with a conspicuous inability to express feeling. 'What a terrible experience for him. Did you . . . did you find out exactly how it happened?'

'Not exactly. We certainly found out when it happened. Tell me, Headmaster: I gather you spoke to the boy earlier on.'

'Pickerage? Not so far as I recollect.'

'The boy who died. Hilary Frome.'

'Ah yes. Hard to think of him as a boy. So mature. So responsible.' The headmaster emitted what sounded like a perfectly genuine sigh. 'This is a bitter blow, Superintendent. A bitter, bitter blow. To myself — and to the School. All the hopes I had . . . How am I going to face his father? What can I tell the other parents?'

'That I can't help you with,' said Pumfrey, his characteristic briskness now almost contemptuous. 'But you say you did speak to Hilary Frome earlier tonight?'

'Yes. Yes, indeed. Oh dear — a melancholy thought. I told him how much pleasure it gave me to think of him in charge of the school next year. As head boy, you know. Who is to take his place I cannot think. Broughton is hardly—'

'Yes, yes,' interrupted Pumfrey impatiently. 'What else did you say to him?'

Mr Crumwallis looked at him in dyspeptic reproof, unused as he was to having his magisterial ramblings interrupted.

'I really . . . don't rememb . . . wait. I think I said how it would please me if one day he were to be elected to the Cullbridge Athenæum. Alas, that will now never be.'

'Did you offer him a drink? Suggest he might like one later?'

'Yes, I did. I . . .'

Suddenly Mr Crumwallis stopped, his eyes popping, fixed in consternation on the Superintendent.

'I suggested he might like a . . . sherry. Oh dear God, Superintendent: don't tell me it was the *sherry*.'

He gazed from the one of them to the other in anguish. And, gazing back, Pumfrey tried to interpret, from his expression, the implications of that last remark. Was it the equivalent of Lady Macbeth's 'What, in our house?' Was he saying 'What, with my sherry?' Or was it to be understood as the horrified realization that, in the words of Hercule Poirot, 'It might have been ME.'

Pumfrey would have given a great deal to know.

CHAPTER 9

MASTER AND SLAVE

'Well,' said Mike Pumfrey, reluctantly dragging his eyes from the spectacle of the headmaster's face. 'I think we'd better look into this a little more closely, don't you? Where do you keep this sherry?'

The headmaster continued gawping dumbly for a second, then without a word he turned on his heel and led the way across the hall. When he opened the door of his sitting-room, Mike Pumfrey saw Mrs Crumwallis, seated bony and straight-backed on a sofa, peering concentratedly at them through her pebble glasses. Pumfrey nodded brusquely in her direction, but there was no response.

'There,' said the headmaster, gesturing uncertainly in the direction of the bottles on the sideboard. 'There they are.'

Pumfrey and Fenniway gazed at them without touching.

'How much is gone, do you know?'

'Really, I can't—'

'*Quite* two glasses full,' said Mrs Crumwallis from the sofa.

'You haven't touched the bottles since you came home? Had a glass yourselves?'

'*No*,' said Mr Crumwallis. 'Thank the Lord. I drink socially if that is necessary, but not otherwise. My wife and I were both brought up Methodists.'

He produced this piece of information with a certain dim self-satisfaction, as if it were a sort of moral American Express card.

'I see,' said Pumfrey. 'Then, supposing the sherry was poisoned, and supposing it was aimed at you, then it could only have been put there by someone who didn't know your habits?'

The headmaster blinked at him owlishly, and then nodded. A thought struck Mike Pumfrey.

'Where were you when you invited Frome to . . . partake?'

'Here. In this room. I called him in from the garden.' The headmaster gestured towards the window, still uncurtained, but giving out on to pitch blackness. 'He had been doing some cricket practice with the younger boarders. Most stylish, a handsome sight . . .' He sighed. 'I called him in, expressed my gratitude at his willingness to hold the fort in the boarding annexe, and then . . . offered him a sherry, if he should feel like it, later on.'

Mrs Crumwallis sniffed.

'Time?' asked Pumfrey.

'Around six-thirty or so, I suppose.

'I see. Were the windows open at the time? Or the door to the hall?'

'Oh—ah—the windows were, yes. The evening was not cold. I believe the door was shut. It usually is.'

'I see. The lower window was open? Yes . . . well, perhaps we could go back to the study. I'll send the prints men down for these.'

He nodded in the direction of the sherry bottles. He could have sworn Mrs Crumwallis had to bite back a demand for the equivalent in money.

Back in the study Edward Crumwallis collapsed into the chair usually reserved for boys whom he was hauling over the coals. The irony did not seem to strike him. In fact, nothing seemed to get through to him at all. He just sat there, gazing at the desk through bleared eyes, but seeming to see nothing. There was no Manner at all to be seen now. He looked a crumbling shell of a man.

'I'm sorry,' he said after a time, struggling to get himself upright in his chair. 'This has struck me very hard . . . Very hard.' In spite of his efforts he seemed to be able to do no more than mumble. 'Who would have thought . . . ?'

'You were fond of the boy?' asked Pumfrey.

'Fond?' said Mr Crumwallis, his forehead crinkling. 'Fond? I had a great *respect* for him. I had great *hopes* for him, and for the school under his leadership. Shattered! Dust and ashes! He would have done us such credit. Now . . .'

'I suppose it was because you had such respect for him that you felt you could leave him in charge of the boarders tonight?'

'Quite. Quite. He'd been a boarder himself—last year when his parents went to the States on three months' sabbatical. I knew I could trust him implicitly. A boy of great rectitude. Of old-fashioned standards.'

'Normally this other young man—Freely, was that the

name?—would have been in charge?'

'Under me. Yes. In charge under me.'

'But tonight he was—?'

'He was accompanying the swimmers. To the All Swessex Schools Championships.' Mike Pumfrey nodded. He had a daughter competing. If he hadn't been on duty he would have been there.

'Is young Freely a swimmer?'

'No, no. Not so far as I know. Our usual man, Muggeridge—' there was a sharp intake of breath, like a suction rubber trying to clear a sink—'an ex-Colchester United player . . . he was unable to accompany them. Family reasons.'

'I see. Yet I gather that Mr Muggeridge was around the school in the grounds tonight.'

The headmaster looked bewildered.

'Really? I'm afraid I don't know anything about that.'

'He would have a key to the school, would he?'

'Oh, certainly.'

'And he could have got into the other parts? Into your quarters? The boarding annexe?'

'Yes. With his keys he could have got into any part.'

'And the other teachers?'

'Oh yes. All of them had keys. In case they had to come back for anything they'd forgotten.'

'But not the boys?'

'Oh no. Not the boys. They couldn't have got into the main part of the school. But they could have got into the boarding annexe. The outer door is not locked until Mr Freely and the older boys go to bed.'

'I see . . .'

'It's a very free and easy place, Superintendent,' said Mr Crumwallis, in an almost pleading voice.

Just plain bloody lax, thought Mike Pumfrey. He did not detect an atmosphere of freedom or ease.

'Now,' he said, 'the members of the staff. I wonder if I

could have a list of them.'

'Ah yes. I — er — I have a prospectus.' Mr Crumwallis fussed round to the front of the desk eagerly, as if Mike Pumfrey were a prospective parent. He took a brochure from the drawer at Pumfrey's right hand, and inspected it. The list had obviously been printed some time before. Some names had been crossed off, as teachers had died at their posts, or departed to more luxuriant scholastic pastures. At the foot of the list new names had been added in ink. Mr Crumwallis, satisfied that it was up to date, handed it to Mike Pumfrey, who inspected it in silence.

Senior English: I. O. McWhirter, B.A. (Durham); B. Litt. (Edinburgh)

Senior Classics: S. G. Coffin, M.A. (Oxon)

Mathematics: P. St. J. Makepeace, M.Sc. (Reading)

Science: C. Farraday, B.Sc. (Kent)

History, French: Miss G. Grower, B.A. (Cantab)

Junior English, History, Geography: Miss D. Gilberd.

Games and Physical Education: W. Muggeridge.

and added in pen:

Junior Classics, French: Miss P. Warlock, B.A. (London)

Head of Boarders: T. Freely (Portlington School; Exhibitioner, Trinity Hall, Cambridge)

Written in days before his present broken state, that last entry seemed to bear the marks of a flourish of self-satisfaction.

'Hmmm,' said Pumfrey. 'You seem to do a lot of classics.'

It was not the remark Mr Crumwallis had been expecting, but he perked up, as he frequently did in interviews with parents, when an opportunity for fraudulent self-congratulation presented itself.

'Yes, indeed,' he said. 'We *lay great* stress on them. So sad to see their decline — their so rapid decline — in other schools, elsewhere. But if the private schools will not be custodians of the great classical tradition, who will be?'

Mike Pumfrey did not feel called upon to reply. He wondered whether, in view of the decline of classics elsewhere, classics teachers might not be in a state of glut upon the market, and therefore to be had cheap. He rather thought they might be. He looked cynically at Mr Crumwallis, swelling with spurious pride.

'Now, this boy, Pickerage . . .'

The head's face immediately fell, as he was brought back to the tribulations of the moment.

'Who? Ah yes, Pickerage. A terrible experience for him. To have to watch . . . *that*.'

'Particularly as I gather he and Frome were friends.'

'Friends? Oh, I don't think so. Hardly likely, Superintendent. Frome was one of our senior boys. We have, alas, no sixth form, but Frome would next year have been in the fifth, and he was old for his years. Pickerage is only in his second year. Oh no, I don't think so.'

Pumfrey marvelled at the limitless naïveté of some schoolteachers.

'What sort of a boy is Pickerage?'

'What sort of a boy?' The question seemed to give the headmaster trouble, as if he was accustomed to regard boys *en masse*, not as individuals. 'He is, perhaps, a shade mischievous. A prankster, shall we say? But we must remember his home background. Or lack of it. His mother—but on that subject, perhaps, the least said the better.'

'You say mischievous. Could you give me some examples?'

'Ah yes. I had occasion, I fear, to slipper the lad only last week. It misgives me now a little, in the circumstances.'

It was the first time Pumfrey had heard anyone use the word 'misgives'. It misgave him no end.

'What had the boy done?'

'He had—I tell you this in confidence, Super-intendent—he had, on the occasion of the annual parents' night, doctored with alcohol the fruit punch intended for the boarders who helped serve the modest refreshments. It was only through my presence of mind that we were saved from a frightful scandal.'

'I see. And you're sure he did it? Did he own up?'

'Not in so many words. But I was morally certain.'

That, thought Pumfrey, was so much flim-flam. Another way of saying 'I had no evidence, but I picked on him.' Policemen who were 'morally certain' someone had done something tended to start manufacturing evidence. Headmasters didn't even have to bother with that.

He wondered whether he should ask Crumwallis to go and sit with the boarders in the dormitory, while he had a word with this young Freely. Freely looked, Pumfrey had thought, honest and sensible. Which would make a change after the headmaster. But Crumwallis in his present state did not look as if he would provide a soothing influence upstairs. Pumfrey decided against it.

'Well, that will be all, for the moment,' he said. 'My men will be here for some time yet, and I'll leave someone here on duty all night. I suggest you try and get some sleep.'

Mr Crumwallis shook his head despairingly.

'I fear not, Superintendent. I . . . fear . . . not.'

And with that final attempt to recapture something of his former Manner, Edward Crumwallis shuffled out of the study. Mike Pumfrey looked at Fenniway and shook his head.

'Silly old buzzard,' he said. 'Aggravating too. If somebody slipped a little cache of something into his plonk, they were probably irritated out of their tiny minds.'

'Is that what you think it was?'

'Could be. The boys, for example, might not know he doesn't drink at home. You know what schools are like—all sorts of rumours get around: this master is a sex-maniac, this one an alcoholic. And they're usually perfectly innocuous chaps. So one of the boys could well have imagined that the Crumwallises knocked it back enthusiastically in the privacy of their home. By the way, did you see the name of the Science teacher here?'

'No,' Fenniway looked at the prospectus. 'C. Farraday? Doesn't mean a thing to me.'

'Corbett Farraday. Enthusiastic naturalist chappie, always writing letters and little pieces for the *Sturford Gazette* about plant species threatened by insecticide, or the medicinal properties of this or that weed. There was an interview not so long ago. I wonder what he's been teaching the boys . . .'

They thought about that for a moment.

'Poisonous properties, and all that?' asked Fenniway. 'Surely he wouldn't be so silly?'

'He looked a young chap, mad keen and so on. That sort does all sorts of silly things, till experience tells them to put a sock in it. Let's hope this isn't the experience . . . Well, no point in going into that until we've heard from the labs. It seems to have acted remarkably quickly, whatever it was. But we've got to remember he seems to have knocked back one while he was down here.'

'When presumably he didn't notice it tasted off,' interjected Fenniway.

'Well, he wouldn't necessarily notice. Alcohol often tastes vile to people who aren't used to it. Funny so many get the taste, really He mayn't have had much before.'

'Today's youngsters?' said Fenniway, sceptically. 'He was practically sixteen, remember. Don't tell me the doctor doesn't have sherry and stuff regularly on tap in the house.'

'Hmmm. See your point. Well, I don't think there's

much more we can do here tonight, but before we wind things up, I think I'd like a word with that lad upstairs. Freely. Looked a sensible, down-to-earth type to me, and he might be a corrective to what we've just been hearing. Do you think you could go upstairs and be with the boys in the dormitory? Someone should be there. I thought of asking that old fool, but I decided he'd probably unsettle them more than calm them down.'

'What do I tell them? About the boy's death. They're bound to be wide awake.'

'Tell them what we know, which is practically nothing. We don't know how he died, but presumably it was something he ate or drank. *Not* supper—emphasize that—or more of them would be affected by now. There's no point in holding that kind of thing back. This is going to be the sensation of the school tomorrow. It's going to be all over town, in fact.'

'I wouldn't like to bet on this school's future,' said Fenniway.

'Nor me. And I wouldn't weep tears over it, either. But let's not hurry the process. Just keep things quiet and unemotional, and talk to the ones who are awake.'

When Toby came in five minutes later, Pumfrey said: 'Things quietening down?'

'A bit,' said Toby. 'Mainly because they're tired, not because they're accepting it. Things are going to be bloody dreadful in the morning.'

'I guess so,' said Pumfrey. 'And not just for the boys either. How did you come to land up in a place like this?'

When Toby had told him, Pumfrey whistled.

'By gum! *No* salary. I like their cheek! Why would you accept it?'

'You may have noticed there's a lot of unemployment about. I had six months to fill in before I go up to Cambridge. I didn't want to do it at school or at home. I get a bed, and food, and a bit of pocket money from the teaching I do when I fill in. It hasn't worked out badly.'

'But it's a lousy school, isn't it?'

Toby considered.

'Yes. I sometimes think most schools are, in different ways. The one I went to certainly was. All penny-pinching and ludicrously outdated snobberies. This one has some pretty dreadful teachers. Makepeace's classes are nothing but advanced courses in riot-fomentation. A lot of the others like McWhirter just don't seem to care. But there are one or two perfectly good teachers as well, so far as I can judge.'

'What about the boys? So far I've only met Pickerage.'

'Pickerage is a fair specimen of the boarders. He's all right. Comes from a pretty awful home, apparently. No father to speak of—he's got a new family, lives in Germany, and doesn't give a damn about Malcolm. The mother flits from flower to flower, and swoops in here on occasional state visits. Terribly embarrassing for the boy. I'm sorry for him. In spite of it all, he's a nice little chap.'

'I gather the headmaster had to slipper him last week.'

'Er—yes,' said Toby.

'Any resentment there?'

Toby was puzzled by the question.

'You mean Pickerage resented the slippering? Good heavens, no. Pickerage doesn't worry about a little thing like that. And he's not the resentful type.'

'But mischievous, I gather. The head said he doctored the fruit cup, or something.'

'So the headmaster believed,' said Toby cautiously.

'You don't?'

'I rather doubt it. If it was just an isolated prank (and he's capable of a prank like that), he would have told me, at least after the slippering. On the other hand, if it was part of something bigger . . .'

'Something bigger?'

'Didn't the headmaster tell you? He should have.

Someone hid a razor blade in the flannel of one of the boarders. It made a fearful mess, though it was only a superficial wound.'

'I saw a boy up there with plaster all down his cheek. That would be him, I take it.'

'Yes, that's Wattling. He's a friend of Pickerage. I do know these boys, Superintendent and I really don't believe Pickerage is capable of anything as vicious as that was. And especially not of aiming it at one of his friends. That was Wattling's flannel, and Pickerage knew he just chucked it at his face every night.'

'I see. I can only take your word for it. In the police force we get cynical about thirteen-year-old boys. We only see the worst, and some of those are fairly horrible, I can tell you. So this seems to be part of a series of incidents . . . or, perhaps, someone taking advantage of a series of incidents. Now, I gather this Hilary Frome was head boy designate, splendid character all round, pink of respectability and model of responsible behaviour. Is that right?'

Toby thought for a moment.

'No,' he said.

'Aaah.' Pumfrey leaned forward, a ferret-like expression on his face. 'Headmaster fooled. Is that it?'

'Pretty much,' admitted Toby.

'Doesn't surprise me. Wouldn't take much, I imagine.'

'No. He and his wife save any sharpness they have for money matters,' said Toby, throwing loyalty to the winds. 'Hilary Frome was in fact riding two horses. All the rest of the staff knew that, and of course the boys knew it too. For the headmaster he did a great act as the old-style schoolboy of the boys' weeklies: "Play up, play up, and play the game," and all that kind of thing. For most of the teachers — Makepeace, for example — he was the one behind any riot, disruption, discontent or whatever. And they were right. He was a stirrer. He was what they used to call a bad influence in the school. I was beginning to be afraid . . .'

'Yes?'

'Well—about Pickerage. Pickerage admired him tremendously. As you can imagine, that's not unusual, especially in boarding-schools. And Hilary had dash, and style, and good looks—all the usual things that make a schoolboy hero. But Hilary not only encouraged this hero-worship, he really seemed to make a friend of Pickerage. Almost a protégé . . .'

'You wondered how far it had gone?'

'Yes. For example, they were together all last Sunday. I knew in advance, but there wasn't much I could do. Pickerage said they were going to Frome's house, but they didn't. So naturally, I suppose, I wondered what they did . . .'

'I see. How would you sum this Frome boy up, then? What was behind this double game? Just mischief?'

'Mischief? He wasn't the mischievous sort, if you mean schoolboy mischief. If you mean something nastier—well, maybe. You've got to remember I didn't know him all that well. I didn't teach him, you see, so the other teachers certainly know him—knew him—better than I did. What I knew I certainly didn't go for. He was a very cold character, I think. Calculating. Really only interested in himself. He seemed to be always looking at himself—not literally, but trying to see what effect he was making. Posing himself against a background, if you see what I mean. He was sort of clinical—trying things out all the time. Like dissecting a frog, only using people and real-life situations. For example, he enjoyed seeing how far he could push the teachers—with concealed insults, fomenting riots, with prying into their private lives. I think if he'd driven poor little Makepeace to a nervous breakdown, his reaction would simply have been "so that's how far one has to go, to have *that* effect." '

'He sounds a right little charmer. I presume that the teachers hated his guts.'

'They loathed him. They—' Toby pulled himself up. 'Well, perhaps you'd better talk to them about that.'

'I will. He certainly seems to have been asking for something, if not something quite as drastic as he got. I presume you weren't enthusiastic about handing the boarders over to him?'

'Naturally I wasn't. I didn't exactly have a presentiment—certainly not of anything like *this* happening. But I didn't like it at all. Trouble was, I'd stood out against Crumwallis earlier this week. When Wattling carved up his face, the head wanted to hand him over to Mrs C., without calling the doctor in.'

'*Really?*'

'And as you'll probably find out, Mrs C.'s ministrations are pretty hit and miss affairs. He just wanted to keep things quiet, obviously. Anything like that, if it gets around, is bad for a school. Bad for recruitment, as you might say. But having got my way over that, it meant I couldn't protest as I wanted to about Frome being put in charge. I didn't even think I could explain what I was afraid of. I didn't think Crumwallis would have understood.'

'I wonder,' said Mike Pumfrey.

When he had sent Toby Freely back to the boarders, he and Fenniway began to collect their things together.

'We might as well call it a night,' said Pumfrey, weariness having settled over his thrusting manner. 'Get a few hours' sleep. It's going to be a hard day tomorrow, and we'll have to be here early. What's it like upstairs? Did you get anything of interest out of them?'

'Not really. It seems to have been a fairly ordinary evening up until the end. Supper, telly, and so on. Then he went off to give Pickerage his medicine. One moment he was shouting at the boys in the dorm to keep quiet, the next thing he was in the bathroom retching, then out on the landing, heaving and crying out. Poor little buggers are going to dream about that for weeks. What have you got the telephone directory out for?'

'Just looking up where this Muggeridge lives . . . Hmmm. Where's Cannonbury Road?'

'Round the back here. I should think if you went across Crumwallis's lawn and through the trees at the back you'd come to it. By road you'd have to drive round, of course, but even so it wouldn't be far.'

'Really? Well, I have a fancy to see it, and I think we might take a look on our way home.'

So they drove round the outskirts of the Burleigh grounds, and eventually came to Cannonbury Road. No. 28, Bill and Onyx's house, was a really shoddy little semi, thrown together by some builder after a quick buck ten or twelve years before. It was bare, basic, meagre: mean little windows slapped planless into the wall, a miserable little square of concrete slapped over the door. In front was a tiny apron of garden, which the street light revealed to be a shambles of children's toys and discarded garments.

The only interesting thing about the house was the top window. Because in it, through a slit in the curtains which had been drawn as incompetently as everything else about the house had been done, a heavy man could be seen, in winceyette pyjamas, red-faced and gesturing angrily. He was shouting at someone or something that could not be seen. Pumfrey let down the car window.

'You bloody tart,' Bill Muggeridge was shouting. 'I know what you were after. You don't usually make much secret of it, do you? If I'd found out where you went I'd have caught you at it.'

He caught sight, through the slit in the curtain, of the

car drawn up outside. He pulled it shut abruptly, and then turned off the light. The policemen heard no more.

'Interesting,' said Pumfrey. And then they drove home.

CHAPTER 10

THE MORNING AFTER

'Through the night of doubt and sorrow
Onward goes the pilgrim band,'

sang the boys of Burleigh School. Presiding from the centre of the dais, Mr Crumwallis looked as if he had told wearily over every second of every minute of the watches of that night. Gowned, dark-suited, he ought to have looked fitting, impressive. But no boy could fail to notice the hollows of his cheeks, which seemed to have been scooped out in deep, dark channels, or his eyes, which were ringed round with black, and bleary, and haunted.

'Brother clasps the hand of brother,
Stepping fearless through the night . . .'

Even the boys didn't sound convinced. The news had spread like the Great Plague as they gathered for Assembly, and underneath the frank, animal sensationalism of their reception of the news there was uncertainty, and fear. Death happened—they were old enough to have acknowledged that. But not to people they knew. Not to friends. Not to people of their age. And *that* sort of death . . . One of the boys in 2B with a good memory had suddenly quoted 'Alas, regardless of their doom the little victims play.' The boys around him had looked at each other, one had laughed uncertainly, another had said, 'Shut up.' Then Mr Crumwallis had walked in.

Edward Crumwallis knew he ought to say something. Say something about the death, about Hilary's death. The thought hovered over him like the onset of a nightmare. What words could he find? What mere formulation could convey his feelings? What if he should break down?

The memory hammered in his head of the dreadful phone call he had made to Dr and Mrs Frome. Both had been at the hospital until after midnight, though they had understood from the moment they arrived that their son was dead. When they had returned home they had disconnected the phone. Now, this morning, Edward Crumwallis had finally spoken to Hilary's father, and the doctor's words rang in his ears:

'I wish to hell I'd never sent him to your school.'

An influential man, Frome. Doctors were always in some way or other community leaders, much more so than lawyers or bankers. And Dr Frome was clearly not willing to smooth over the terrible event, to refrain from raking over the coals. He sounded, indeed, vindictive. Perhaps somewhere in the back of Edward Crumwallis's brain there ran a murmur telling him that Dr Frome had every right to be.

Now, if ever, between hymn and prayer, something ought to be said about Hilary. Something brief, dignified and reverent. Something to raise the spirits of the boys, to still speculation.

'Then, the scattering of all shadows,
And the end of toil and gloom.'

Mr Crumwallis cleared his throat. It was no good. Nothing would come.

'Let us pray,' he said.

It was his first capitulation of the day.

*

Dr Frome said exactly the same thing, sitting beside his wife, in the living room of *Deauville*, Maple Grove, when he was interviewed by Mike Pumfrey and Fenniway.

'I wish to hell I'd never sent him there.'

It was after nine o'clock, but Dr Frome's smooth good looks were marred by stubble and red eyes. His wife's hair was straggling over her eyes, and she had not made up to hide the ravages of the night's events. Not a particularly admirable pair, Pumfrey decided, but at least one that cared. Or seemed to have.

'Why did you?' asked Pumfrey.

'Send him to Burleigh?' John Frome put his head in his hands. 'I don't know . . . It was four years ago, and that was when it was clear that they couldn't hold out against comprehensivisation any longer. As you know, they dug in their heels here longer than practically anywhere else, but in the end they caved in. We couldn't quite run to a good boarding-school, so we chose Burleigh.'

'There was the little girl, too, you see,' said Mrs Frome. 'She's going to St Mary's. And that's not cheap, unless you're very poor, and Catholic.'

'Worst damn decision I ever made,' said John Frome, straightening himself and blinking his eyes.

'Hilary knew,' said Mrs Frome. 'He always said it was neither one thing nor the other. We should have listened.'

'If only they hadn't scrapped the old grammar school,' muttered Dr Frome, and Pumfrey saw that he was beginning to erect in his mind a structure of excuses and evasions that would justify him to himself. 'I'd have been quite happy with that.'

Mike Pumfrey cleared his throat. Comprehensivisation, he muttered to himself, seemed to have had much the same effect on the middle-middle class in England as racial integration in schools had had on similar people in the States. Normally he would have had little patience with the attitudes of the Fromes, but the morning after such a bereavement didn't seem the time to argue the social or political toss with them. For once he was almost gentle.

'Yet according to the headmaster Hilary was a most successful boy at school,' he said. 'About to become head boy, and so on.'

'Yes . . . yes . . .' agreed Dr Frome, tiredly. 'We bought all that too. That's why we decided to keep him there. He's good with the soft soap, is Crumwallis. That's why we told Hilary he'd have to stay for GCE year. Though we knew some of the teaching was abysmal.'

'That pathetic little Makepeace,' said Mrs Frome. 'Like a church mouse. Hilary just despised him.'

'And the science teaching was pretty poor, too,' said her husband. 'Maths and science— just the subjects Hilary would need if he was going to be a doctor. I was giving up a great deal of my own time, I may say, just to supplement the inadequate teaching he got at Burleigh. Ridiculous . . . Time thrown away— now.'

'Did you want him to become a doctor?'

'It was a possibility. One of the options. But you've got to be first-rate academically to get into medical school. Hilary always said he'd never make it, not from Burleigh . . . He was also interested in Communications . . . He was a very personable boy, Superintendent. People responded to him. Respected him. He could have gone anywhere, done anything.'

'So the headmaster said,' agreed Pumfrey cautiously. 'What about his friends? Did he have any especially close ones?'

'Well, there was young Willis,' said Mrs Frome, who had been quietly rubbing her eyes with a small handkerchief. 'He was round here now and then. And Peter Quigly. Both very nice types. We know the parents socially. And he had such a nice little girlfriend . . . Well, not *girlfriend*, because he was too young, but . . . you know. Margaret Wilkinson was her name. Very nicely spoken. But we don't know the parents there, do we, John? And we hadn't heard so much about her recently, anyway.'

'This boy Pickerage, who he was with when—just before he died. Had you heard of him?'

'Was that the boy in the sick bay? No, I'd never heard Hilary mention him,' said Mrs Frome. But she suddenly puckered her forehead. 'But I have heard the name . . . That's right: someone rang up and asked for him the other day. But he wasn't a friend of Hilary's, not so far as I know.'

Frome had been sitting quiet, looking down at his hands. At length he spoke.

'How did it happen, Superintendent? Do you know yet?'.

'No. There won't be anything substantial from the labs for a few hours yet. We do know that the headmaster spoke to him early in the evening, and suggested he might like a glass of sherry later on—'

'Sherry? You mean the headmaster offered his own sherry? What a damnfool thing to do.'

'And we know that Hilary did go and get himself one.'

'So it could have been the headmaster who—?'

'We're trying not to draw conclusions this early on, sir. How used was your son to drink?'

'Well, of course, just the occasional one, on special occasions,' chipped in Mrs Frome, almost defensively. 'Like Christmas, and birthdays, and occasionally out with us in the evening. We hoped he would drink in a *civilized* way.'

'So he went down,' said Frome, as if puzzling it out, 'and he helped himself to the headmaster's sherry.'

'That's right. We know too that he took a glass from the medicine cupboard in the sick bay.'

Dr Frome slapped himself violently on the thigh.

'That's it! I knew it! My God! I blame myself — a doctor. I knew perfectly well that woman was a menace. Supposed to be matron, and knew no more than a charwoman. Less. Prescribed all sorts of rubbish — just willynilly. I thought it just *was* rubbish, and couldn't do any harm. But she'd no idea of method, hygiene — anything. I bet there was something left in that glass.'

'It's a possibility, and we've thought of that. We certainly have the impression that Mrs Crumwallis is not the person to treat sick boys. Now, I wonder if I might trouble you. I'd like to see Hilary's room.'

Heavily, bitterly, the Fromes led the way upstairs. In the door leading to the kitchen Pumfrey noticed a girl of ten or so. She was regarding them with wide, dark eyes, full of uncertainty. But the eyes were quite dry, and not red.

Hilary Frome's bedroom — ample, handsomely decorated, as befitted the solidly middle-class status of the family residence — was as studiously bland as the face Hilary kept for public occasions. It was unnaturally neat, and it carefully refrained from revealing any signs of individuality. There were school books, and one or two old Enid Blytons, but no sign of current reading tastes, nor any well-thumbed magazines. On the wall was a framed Miró. What kind of boy, Pumfrey marvelled, would choose a picture like that to decorate his room? When he left he took a pile of exercise books, a scrapbook and a diary, but a first glance at their contents did not suggest that they were going to be fruitful.

The wide, dry eyes followed them from the kitchen as they took their leave.

When they arrived back at Burleigh the hallway of the headmaster's quarters was a mass of whispering groups. Tom Tedder and Corbett Farraday were muttering by the door which led into the main school; the headmaster, towering yet crumpled, was surrounded by a little group of teachers in the centre of his hall; and by the door leading to the boarding quarters Mrs Crumwallis was going over the events of the night before with her cook, Mrs Garfitt.

' 'Eaving up, was he?' said that lady, licking her fat lips with ghoulish relish. 'Throwing up and 'olding 'is stomach? Sounds like something 'e het, don't it? Nothing from *my* kitchen, anyway. What 'appened then?'

'Then he died,' said Mrs Crumwallis. She seemed to lack any Dickensian sense of the poetry of death.

'Fancy. Died. There on your lap. 'Orrible for you, Mrs C. But he always was very white and fair, wasn't 'e? Some'ow you can imagine 'im as one of those marboreal effigies in church. Tell me again what 'appened when you got 'ome. The shepherd's is unfreezing, so there's no rush for lunch. You got 'ome, and you 'eard sounds, is that it?'

The headmaster's little group of himself, Septimus Coffin and Penny Warlock was joined by Mr McWhirter, limping late into school on his way to his first class. Catching wind of the disturbance, he poked his head around the door and in his early-morning voice, like a flute with catarrh, he threw the inquiry in the direction of Mr Crumwallis.

'Something wrong, eh?'

'Yes,' said Mr Crumwallis in an undertaker's voice. 'A boy has died.'

'Oh, is that all?' Mr McWhirter began a painful right turn, but then a thought struck him. 'Which one?'

'Alas—it was Hilary Frome.'

'Ha! Really? Ha! No great loss.'

The headmaster, ignoring Mr McWhirter's privileged position, was about to enter a stinging demurrer when the phone rang.

Mr Crumwallis froze.

'The telephone again.'

His voice was that of a breaking man. He walked with palpable reluctance in the direction of his sitting-room. Septimus Coffin cast a brief glance towards Iain McWhirter. Then the various groups, still muttering anxiously to each other, began to evaporate in various directions. Mike Pumfrey, now back in the study with Sergeant Fenniway, put his finger to his lips and picked up the extension phone.

'My dear Mr Martins, I *beg* you to reconsider, to make no hasty decision,' came the headmaster's voice, raised to a sort of wail that was anything but confidence-creating. 'I feel sure this thing will turn out to be an unfortunate accident . . . Well, it's all very well to say that accidents like that shouldn't happen, but . . . Naturally you don't want to take risks with your boy, I can see that perfectly well, but—'

Mike Pumfrey laid the receiver down gently, and raised his eyebrows at Fenniway.

'Not the first today, I'd be willing to bet.'

'Nor the last,' said Fenniway.

Never had morning worn on more agonizingly slowly. Never, even at Burleigh School, had less been taught.

Pumfrey, respecting the routine of the school, though there was little enough cause to, interviewed the teachers when they had a free period. Bill Muggeridge, he noted with regret, had been free for the first hour, when Pumfrey and Fenniway had been busy with the Fromes, but was not free again until after lunch. The rest were available at one time or another. The first to come, and one of the most interesting from Pumfrey's point of view, was Tom Tedder, who sprawled easily in his chair, seemed as little tensed up as it is possible to be when involved in a murder case, and told them all they needed to know about the teachers' attitude to the school's star pupil.

'Frightful little shit,' he said. 'And it didn't help his being the headmaster's publicly proclaimed "boy most likely". That just gave him the more confidence.'

'Confidence to do what?'

'Oh, raising riot and rebellion in the usual schoolboy way. He *was* only a schoolboy, after all: we all tended to forget that. But there was something more with Frome. The way he needled the staff, for example. Picked on their weakest points, twisted the knife . . .'

'Yes. Who are you thinking of?'

'Most of us, really. Makepeace, of course, was easy game. But he'd take on someone like Glenda Grower, who's a much tougher customer. Make some snide remark about what happened in her last school.'

'Oh. And what did happen?'

'Some ghastly little girl accused her of lesbian advances.'

'And is she a lesbian?'

'Personally I'd guess not. Since the women's movement started bringing all the lesbians out, anyone with a bit of presence gets accused of it. And Glenda's certainly got presence. As I say, I'd guess not, but she never talks about it, and nobody'd dare bring it up. Except Hilary Frome.'

'I see. What else did he throw at you teachers?'

'Oh, he said something to poor Miss Gilberd the other day.' He stopped. 'At least, he may have done.'

'Why are you unsure?'

'Well, at the time—' he stopped, embarrassed, but saw he was in too far—'I thought she might have . . . have made it up. Well, I'd better tell you. I thought she might have made it up as an excuse for coming round to see me. She wouldn't tell me exactly what he'd said. But in fact, he seemed to have quite a campaign going against the staff, so he might easily have said something.'

'What sort of thing would he have said?'

'Oh, something about her and me. Poor old Dorothea

thinks it's a state secret, but in fact everybody giggles over it.'

'I see. And what about you, sir?'

'Me? Oh, I don't take the older boys, or only the dimmer ones in the lower streams. I hadn't had Hilary since he was in the second year.'

'So he'd never done anything special to you?'

Tom Tedder remembered one morning, four years back, when he had taken into class a picture he had painted, and rather liked—a picture of Florence from Fiesole. He remembered the admiring glances of the other boys, and the expression of ineffable contempt on the face of the young Hilary Frome, an expression that told him that even an eleven-year-old could see through him, could tell he was no good.

'No. He never said anything special to me,' he said. 'His general foulness didn't ripen till later.'

The progressive questioning of the staff made for a terrible atmosphere in the Staff Common Room. Indeed, if they had thought about it, it would have been all too ludicrously reminiscent of being called up before the headmaster.

'Well,' said Dorothea Gilberd, coming in sweaty and harassed from a Geography class with 1A, 'there's certainly no prospect of getting anything done today.'

'Weally?' said Mr Makepeace. 'I found 4A tewibly quiet.'

'I don't wonder. That's Hilary Frome's class. They would be. That doesn't mean they're taking anything in.'

'Oh, I don't ask for miwacles. Who's with the Superintendent at the moment?'

'McWhirter, I think,' said Dorothea. 'Tom went first,' she said, artlessly revealing what was on her mind. 'I haven't seen him since. What's the man asking us about?'

'Where we were yesterday after school,' said Glenda

Grower, apparently little concerned. 'And what were our impressions of Hilary Frome.'

'He asked me if I'd been teaching them about poisonous plants,' said Corbett Farraday. 'As if I would! Of course, we did do some elementary botany . . .'

'Hmmm,' said Septimus Coffin. 'And on the subject of Hilary, what is the party line? Are we being honest?'

'Well, I was, in moderation,' said Glenda. 'The funny thing is, I felt rather rotten about telling him what I thought of Hilary. I mean, the boy was only fifteen or sixteen. He was a ghastly little tyke, but it is quite awful that he's dead. People who are little horrors in school quite often grow up into all right individuals.'

'And *vice versa*, of course,' said Septimus Coffin. 'The point about one's schooldays is that they are the most irrelevant days of one's life.'

'Don't talk rubbish, Sep,' said Dorothea briskly. 'If you thought that, you wouldn't be a schoolteacher . . . Oh dear, I wonder what Tom told them.'

'Why? Does he have anything to tell them?'

Dorothea blushed, as if automatically.

'No, of course not. And luckily we've both got a very good alibi for last night. I . . . I happened to have an extra ticket for the recital last night . . . Holmes, the violinist, you know . . . and I rang up Tom on the off-chance that he'd like to come.'

Glenda Grower, out of sheer mercy, changed the subject.

'Alibi,' she said. 'I notice you're all assuming that the boy was murdered. Aren't we jumping the gun a bit? I bet the Superintendent hasn't made up his mind about that yet, not judging by the tone of his questions.'

'My boys in 1A aren't convinced of it either,' chipped in Dorothea gratefully. 'They'd like it to be murder, because that would be more sensational, and they'd like to see someone dragged off, but they really think it was an accident. They haven't worked it out yet, but they're sure it's something to do with Mrs C. and her damned medicines.'

'They have a point,' said Glenda. 'Precisely what I think.'

'Hmmm,' said Septimus Coffin. 'If it is . . .'

They all looked at him inquiringly.

'I pwesume,' said Percy Makepeace, 'you think that would be the end of Burleigh.'

'Not exactly,' said Septimus. 'I think it would be the end of Crumwallis at Burleigh.'

'What's this, Sep?' said Tom Tedder, coming in from his last class, and acting rather as if a load was now off his mind, or as if he was trying to conceal one. "Writing off the Crumwallises already?'

'Only,' said Coffin judiciously, 'in certain circumstances.'

'Like his lovely lady wife having inadvertently poisoned off his star pupil, you mean? No, it wouldn't exactly foster confidence, would it? Actually the idea that that's what happened has probably got round the parents already. Boys talk, you know, and everyone was aware of her medicinal vagaries. Mr C. is looking like Dr Jekyll after a nasty spell as Mr Hyde, by the by. *And* he's on the phone again.'

'Really?' said Septimus Coffin. And before long he drank up his coffee and slipped out.

'Tom,' said Dorothea urgently, 'what was it like? What did he ask you about?'

'Same as everyone else, I should think. Where I was last night, and so on. I told him about the concert.'

'Was that all?'

'Then he wanted to know what I thought of young Hilary,' said Tom. He swallowed, as if making a decision. 'I told him that as far as I was concerned he was junior shit of all time. I — er — I told him about his insulting you.'

'Oh Tom—' wailed Dorothea. 'You *didn't*!'

'Well, after all, what's the odds? He needs to know what a ghastly little prick the boy was. The headmaster would never tell him, and most of this lot will pull their punches. And we've got perfect alibis.'

But Dorothea Gilberd was not to be comforted.

'I don't know that alibis are all that much use,' she said. 'Not in poison cases.'

'But Mrs Quigly,' shouted the headmaster down the phone, oblivious in his desperation of the fact that his sitting-room door was slightly ajar, 'I will not be condemned without trial in this way . . . Yes, I realize you are under no obligation to keep Peter here. But I think I can say that we have never betrayed the trust that you have reposed in us . . . That is a most unwarranted slur . . . My wife has never laid claim to medical knowledge, Mrs Quigly . . . I must beg you to take a few days to con*sid*er . . . All this will be sorted out, perhaps in a matter of hours . . . Mrs Quigly! Mrs Quigly!'

He stood by the fireplace, gazing despairingly at the mouthpiece of the telephone. It was at this point that the door swung open.

'I think, Mr Crumwallis,' said Septimus Coffin, marching in, 'that we'd better sit down and have a really good talk.'

CHAPTER 11

DECLINE AND FALL

'But that's hardly more than I paid for it!' protested Edward Crumwallis, his voice high with outrage and fear. 'Allowing for inflation, it's very much less than I paid for it.'

'Quite,' said Septimus Coffin.

'It's an unthinkable proposition. You take no account of the way I have built the school up.'

'Oh, I do,' said Septimus Coffin. 'And also of the way it is currently collapsing about your ears.'

'Nonsense! Fiddlesticks! A temporary setback.'

'Oh no. This school will never recover as long as you and your wife are here. Unfair, perhaps, but there it is. Even if Frome's death has nothing to do with your wife's . . . ministrations, the word has spread now. One thing parents can't afford — especially our sort of parent — is that the whisper might be put about that they had been willing to toy with their own children's safety. Just wait and see: that phone will ring again within the next ten minutes.'

Mr Crumwallis jumped, and looked nervously at the instrument.

'But what would we do?'

'That's rather up to you, isn't it? Retire gracefully for a time. Then quietly buy another school. I've known teachers go on to other posts in the private sector without any trouble after far worse things than you will ever be accused of. Or why not try some other kind of institution? A private nursing home for old people, for example. Under proper medical supervision, of course.'

'You are being intolerably insulting. I'd like to know what your interest in this is, and McWhirter's.'

'Iain Ogilvie McWhirter, like the good Scot he is, wants to protect the capital he's already invested. He doesn't see any way of doing that as long as you and Mrs C. remain here. I'm like the rest: I want to preserve my job. At the moment it looks as if the end of term will see us all thrown on the job market. Not a happy prospect. You know what the outlook is for unemployed teachers at the moment.'

'I don't see why you care,' whined the headmaster. 'Not at your age.'

'It's precisely because of my age that I can be quite sure there won't be any other job coming my way if I lose this one. Well, now, you've had our offer—McWhirter's and mine. This offer does not go up. It goes down.'

'What do you mean?' said Mr Crumwallis, the note of fear back in his voice as if he understood already perfectly well.

'This is a business deal—right? Or as you would say, a commercial transaction. Just like the deal *you* made when you bought the school. Strict commercial principles operate—the market economy. Every time that phone rings the future of this school looks more and more shaky. Every parent who withdraws his boy is going to increase our difficulties, and make it less likely we'll get other boys to take their places. We're willing to try it. But every hour you hang on makes it more risky. That's why every hour the offer will go down.'

'I take this most unkindly, Coffin. Most unkindly. You seem to have no sense of gratitude. It was I, you remember, who offered you a position here.'

'At a salary less than I was earning twenty years ago in the State system. Gratitude had nothing to do with it, as Mae West didn't say. Right—now give me your answer: yes or no?'

'No. Certainly not . . . I have no intention of . . . this is pure blackmail . . . Taking advantage of a temporary situation . . . A piece of rank treachery—'

Mr Crumwallis jumped a foot when the telephone rang. Septimus Coffin, with a little bow of the head, retired and left him to it.

The bell for lunch was going when Mike Pumfrey and Sergeant Fenniway finished the main part of their initial interviews. Only Muggeridge was still unseen. Pumfrey sat back in his chair and his thin face, with its alert blue eyes and the bristly little moustache, assumed the look of a frustrated ferret.

'Well, here's the picture, for what it's worth,' he said. 'Percival Makepeace drove to the Church of St Athelwold the Martyr at Little Tunbury on the Mere. To inspect their incomparable rood screen—or woood screen, as he called it. I wondered what the hell he meant, and I'm still not sure. Twies to visit it once a year, at the vewy least. Well, well. Saw nobody. Surprise, surprise. Drove back to a late dinner. No alibi. Septimus Coffin went home at four-fifteen. Read the paper, ate, listened to music, watched the television with his sister. A sort of alibi for the whole time.'

'But that's pretty much a wife's alibi, isn't it?' said Sergeant Fenniway. 'Not a great deal of use. And his sister is sixty-eight. Old people go to sleep in front of the television.'

'Don't we all? Yes, it's a pretty shaky alibi when you come down to it. Next, Corbett Farraday was home, at afternoon tea with his mama (who sounds a formidable body, not to say a right old battleaxe). Then he went walking in Stanhope Wood, looking for a root of something Latin and nasty-sounding, which might be interesting when we know what Frome died of, except that if it was Corbett Farraday he would hardly flourish the matter so gaily in our faces, naïve as he certainly seemed to be.

Penelope Warlock and Glenda Grower were both at home,
marking. The first rang the second at nine-fifteen — not
long before Hilary Frome died. In effect, no alibi. Iain
Ogilvie McWhirter—'

'There's a character. Like a dried vegetable, or something. I bet his lessons sparkle.'

'Quite. A machine for teaching, and — like all British
industrial plants — a pretty much obsolete one at that.
Part owner of the school, though, you notice. Which
doesn't alter the fact that he has no alibi. At home
working on his *Dictionary of Gaelic on Historical
Principles*, and struggling with *The Times Literary
Supplement* crossword. Wife away on a visit to her
mother. Only child, a daughter at Oxford. But why
someone like that would want to endanger his own
property by killing off one of the boys is beyond me.'

'Tedder and Miss Gilberd have the best alibis,' said
Fenniway.

'From seven forty-five onwards, yes. Unbreakable, I
imagine. But *if* something was slipped into the sherry, *if*
Crumwallis was overheard talking to Frome, it could have
been earlier. For the period around six to seven-thirty
Tedder had no alibi at all, and Miss Gillberd only her
ancient mother.'

'That leaves Muggeridge. There's something odd there,
sir, but we've no more than a whiff of what it was. And,
talking to these teachers, I can't for the life of me see what
motive any of them can have. Quite apart from anything
else, the most likely immediate consequence for them is
that they lose their jobs.'

'No small thing, these days. And yet, they hated him.
Crumwallis, apparently, excepted. Crumwallis — I would
bet — was sexually attracted, whether he understood that
himself, or not. Otherwise they hated him, though there
are degrees of honesty as to how far they admit it.'

'Still,' said Fenniway, 'if schoolteachers went around

killing off the kids they hate—'

'I probably wouldn't be here myself. I was a little demon, I can tell you. One of them called me Hitler, do you know that? And that was fifteen years before I grew this moustache.' Pumfrey fingered that little bunch of bristles in fond reflection. 'And yet, you know, there's surely more than just hatred for a disruptive influence in class. The thing between him and the staff got pretty personal at times. In due course we might look closer at that episode with the Gilberd: she admits after much blushing and prevarication that he accused her in the High Street delicatessen of baby-snatching—did it openly, in a loud voice. Now Gilberd seemed eminently sane—I know the type so well from my schooldays, and that type always kept me perfectly well under control. But there might be other, more dangerous examples of his getting personal, and with people who are not so well balanced. The type of teacher you get in a school like this is often enough a screwball, an outsider, or so I should guess. The type that can't get a job in the State system, or has lost one. Makepeace, for example—what's under that timid exterior? Then there's Miss Grower. According to Tedder, she was apparently accused of lesbian advances by a girl at her old school.'

'But she's hardly blackmailable over that, sir. It's apparently well known.'

'Certainly. But there could have been other episodes, involving local girls. And Frome could easily have heard, if they were around his own age . . . It's all so nebulous. On the surface I agree: the teachers are not likely. A boy would have better opportunities—of doing that nasty trick with the razor blade, for example. I suppose I'm reluctant to go into the school side before I have to because I'm not very good with kids.'

'Aren't you, sir?'

'No. With my own kids, yes. The funny thing is, all

other kids kind of merge into one grey mass: one boy in a school uniform is the mirror image of the next boy in school uniform. My kids have plenty of friends, and I can't tell one from another, or remember their names. My wife is always going on to me about it. Ah well, we've got one more card before we come to the boys. Could you go along and get this Muggeridge character?'

On the way to the Staff Common room Fenniway had a word with the constable who was taking up Pickerage's lunch, so it was well into lunch break by the time Bill was called. He had begun to wonder whether they might not have forgotten him entirely.

Bill had heard the news that morning when he arrived at school. He had simply said, 'Oh Gawd', but he had certainly looked aghast. Since then his heart had not been in the horse vaulting or the running on the spot. But as it never really was, the boys had not noticed the difference. They did notice that, contrary to his usual custom, he showered at the end of the morning's gym classes; but since he put on the same grubby and sweaty old clothes he had come in, that was practically a wasted gesture. Still, a shower perks you up. When he was fetched from the Common Room his walk had a touch of spring, and he came into Pumfrey's presence a shade more jauntily than would have been the case if he had been interviewed earlier.

'Ah, Mr Muggeridge,' said Pumfrey in a businesslike tone. 'You're the only teacher now that I haven't seen.'

'Had classes all morning,' said Bill. 'You can't leave the little blighters alone in the gym. Not with all that equipment. Ruddy little vandals, the lot of them.'

'Yes, I can see that. I suppose you've got a lot of valuable stuff there. Now, I gather you had to cry off taking your team to the Swimming Championships at Sturford last night.'

'Well, not to say cry off,' said Bill, settling down cosily

with a grievance, like a feminist about to discourse on rape. 'Don't see it's my bloody job anyway, not evening work like that. They just assume I'll go, and he doesn't hand out a penny extra, not old Crumwallis. All bloody unpaid overtime, this job. If we had a union worth anything they'd look into it.'

'But it was assumed you'd do it,' said Pumfrey, cutting into his whinge, or his tactical ramblings, whichever they were. 'However, you said you couldn't go. Why was that?'

'Had to stay at home to mind the kids,' said Bill promptly. 'You know how it is. The Missus had to go out.'

'The Missus' was about as inappropriate a soubriquet for Onyx Muggeridge as could be imagined, and Mike Pumfrey, who had heard a few scraps about her already, registered this.

'Ah — your wife had to go out, so you had to stay home with the children?'

'Yes, like I said. We've got four. All nippers.'

'I see. You couldn't have got a baby-sitter?'

'Why the hell should we? All costs bleeding money, doesn't it?'

'Yes, of course. But, now: were you at home with the children all evening? From the time you left school here?'

'Yes. We had a bit of a fry-up. Then the Missus went out, and I stayed home with the kids. I tell you, they're nippers. Can't leave them — they get up to anything.'

'And yet, we're told that you were seen around the grounds of Burleigh yesterday evening.'

'Seen? 'Course I wasn't. I was home.'

The first beads of sweat appeared on Bill Muggeridge's forehead.

'Are you sure? You were seen by one of the boarders.'

'Bloody little liar. Or else he was mistaken. That was probably it. It was nearly dark.'

'When was it nearly dark, Mr Muggeridge?'

Pumfrey reflected comfortably that it was an indi-

cation of Bill Muggeridge's general dimness that he had
not even had to set a trap for him. He had made the most
ancient blunder in the business quite off his own bat. He
stumbled on.

'I mean, it was probably too dark for him to see. It's
easy to mistake people if it's half light.'

'Come off it, Muggeridge. You've just landed yourself
in it. Why don't you come clean and tell the truth?'

'What do you mean? I am telling the truth. Look — I've
just remembered, I did take a walk — just to get a breath
of fresh air.' Muggeridge once again assumed that
aggrieved air, which was easy enough for him, because he
felt aggrieved much of the time. 'I needed it. Cooped up
in the house like that — stinks of babies the whole time. I'd
rather live near a fish factory than that. Chap's got to get
out, if he's used to fresh air. Went for a walk around the
school, about half past seven or so. My house is just across
the way here.'

'I know where your house is, Muggeridge.' Mike Pumfrey leant sharply forward, and caught Bill's shifty eye.
'We heard you from your bedroom window, when we
called round last night. You called your wife a tart, which
is your business and hers, but you also said that if you'd
known where she'd gone you would have caught her at it.
And that could very well be our business as well as yours.
Come along, Muggeridge, let's have a bit of detail.'

'You crappy sods!' fumed Muggeridge. 'Going round at
dead of night, eavesdropping on people's conversations.
Like damned Peeping Toms. Bet you get a cheap thrill
out of that sort of thing, don't you? You'd arrest anyone
else who did it. That your idea of detective work?'

'Perhaps when you've got over your pet, you'll give us
some answers.'

Bill considered. Considering, for Bill, took time. He
looked like a particularly lethargic Newfoundland dog,
trying to decide whether to obey an order.

'Oh well,' he said, going as always for the muddly middle way, and hoping to struggle along it to safety. 'I suppose it's no skin off my nose. I was looking for my wife.'

'Quite,' said Pumfrey. 'We gathered that.'

He sat back in his chair, with an air of waiting, and expecting something more to the point.

'Well, she'd got a date with someone. She'd ringed off the date on the calendar in the kitchen. Always does that, nasty little bitch. It's her way of telling me, and saying "What are you going to do about it?" I followed her. But the trouble is, it's not something I'm trained at, and I'm heavy. I had to keep well behind her, and then I lost her. She came into the school grounds, I'm pretty sure she crossed the headmaster's lawn, but after that I lost her.'

'What did you do?'

'I went back home. Wasted effort.'

'I see, just like that, eh? Hardly worth missing the swimming for. You say she always ringed that calendar, is that right? Presumably this has happened before, then?'

'Ever open door,' muttered Bill, dredging up one of the more attractive phrases from his footballing past.

'And did you always do the Indian scout job?' asked Pumfrey very quietly. 'Or this time were you more worried than before?'

'Well—she came into the school grounds. I thought it might be with a boy. I wouldn't put it past her, mucky little bint. And that would be serious. It's not much of a job, but these days I wouldn't want to get the push.'

'You thought it might be with a boy. Which boy?'

'How would I know? Any boy.'

Pumfrey looked at him with contempt. Really, Muggeridge was one of the worst and most transparent liars he had ever encountered. Which might be a powerful argument for his essential innocence. Pumfrey didn't have the impression that the killer of Hilary Frome was both clumsy and stupid.

'You give me the gripes,' he said dispassionately. 'I don't like to be taken for an idiot. Do I have to spell it out for you? You must have decided to follow her before she went into the school grounds, because otherwise you wouldn't have opted out of the swimming. You obviously did so because you suspected she was going with one of the boys. You must have seen her with one of them. Which one was it?'

Bill Muggeridge swallowed. This sort of inquisition hadn't happened to him since his schooldays, since he had been the playground bully whose only fear in life was a particularly sharp-eyed and sharp-tongued headmaster. He felt at bay, like a very dim minister facing a hostile House. Unlike the minister, he finally decided to tell the truth.

'Hilary Frome,' he said.

'Aaah—' said Mike Pumfrey, and he leaned forward again, playing with his pen. It was a sign, generally, that the inquisition was just starting. It was a sign that, today, was to be proved false.

The scream came from quite a way away, but it penetrated easily the thick walls of the study. All three men jumped in their seats, and Mike Pumfrey and Fenniway were on their feet in a second and through the door. As they reached the hallway, another scream resounded through the school—a woman's voice? Or could it be a boy's? It came through the door leading to the boarders' annexe. The policemen were first through, but following close on their heels came others—the headmaster from his sitting-room, teachers from their common room. A third scream told them where to go.

The door to the dining hall stood open. No one was sitting down. Mrs Crumwallis and Mrs Garfitt had run from the serving table and were standing over a boy. Both seemed helpless, and Mrs Garfitt was working up to hysterics. Crouched over the end of the table, a boy was heaving up blood—a hideous red pool, soaking into the bare boards of the floor. His face, between heaves, was piteous and terrified.

'Fenniway—ambulance, quick,' said Pumfrey. 'At once. The rest of you, keep away from him.'

And Pumfrey went forward, hardly knowing what to do. He sat the boy on a seat and looked down his throat. There was, at the back, a deep gash.

The headmaster stood, helpless and horrified, by the door. He seemed to be contemplating the magnitude of his own fall. Two days ago—one day ago—he had been in charge of his destiny. A man of power. A man admired, respected, whose word was heeded. Now . . . He looked around pathetically. What he saw was Septimus Coffin.

'The offer,' said the gentleman, 'has gone down by five thousand pounds.'

'Done,' said Edward Crumwallis. And then he amended it with a feeble trace of his old Manner: 'I accept your offer.'

CHAPTER 12

TAKEOVER

Septimus Coffin enjoyed the subsequent afternoon more keenly than he had enjoyed any day in his life since he retired. He was, naturally, properly concerned about the injured boy: phoned the hospital, indeed, several times to ascertain that he was out of danger, and could expect nothing worse than a period of extreme discomfort. But, for the rest, he savoured most intensely the joys of taking over high command, of initiating action, of doing things that, during a lifetime of subordination, he had known headmasters ought to do, but had seldom witnessed them doing.

The race, in the world of education, is seldom to the best-equipped. Headmasters, professors, principals of colleges are seldom appointed because they have qualities that would make them good headmasters, professors or principals of colleges. They are appointed on the basis of quite arbitrary criteria laid down by educational administrators at one level of the bureaucracy or another — failed teachers, often enough, these administrators, and tender towards their kind; or pen-pushers who, because they could not themselves in a month of Sundays recognize what might make for a successful leader, demanded instead all sorts of paper evidence that had no bearing on the case one way or the other.

Septimus Coffin had seen men appointed headmaster, appointed over him, on the basis of little papers they had read to conferences of educators on word acquisition by seven-year-old Kenyan Asians in some undesirable suburb of Birmingham, or on the basis of some windy rubbish they had written for *The Times Educational Supplement* on the place of community studies in sixth-form syllabuses. But Septimus, who would have made a good headmaster, had none of the little bits of paper necessary to argue his case before the Judgment Seat of the educational bureaucracy. He had ended his career at the Grammar School, at about the time it had merged with the other schools of the town to become Cullbridge Comprehensive, as nothing more than senior Classics Master.

Now, belated but sweet, had come his opportunity.

He seized it with admirable firmness and sound judgment. He did, in fact, what Mr Crumwallis would have done had he had the instincts of a headmaster, instead of merely a headmasterly façade. He acted on the principle (beloved of Israeli generals) of the pre-emptive strike. Or, to put it another way, he adopted the slogan of the casting director: 'Don't ring us, we'll ring you.' He made a list—indeed, he had made it earlier—of the twenty most influential parents (clergymen, bankers, lawyers and also some people of genuine moral probity). He rang up each of them in turn and announced to them in a dignified but neutral tone the changed dispensation at Burleigh School. He set out the guidelines on which he intended to run the school; he itemized the reforms, particularly in the medical and catering departments, that he was initiating 'as from today'; he described the teaching standards that he was insisting upon 'as a matter of priority'. He used these phrases somewhat cynically, knowing that they would appeal.

He rang, too, the parents who had already signified their intention of removing their boys. With them he adopted a more supplicatory tone, and secured from several of them a promise that they would hold their hand, or at least think over their decision. He looked over the applications for the post of matron that had come in when it was last advertised, decided on the most qualified, got her on the phone and offered her the salary she demanded. She promised to be on hand from nine o'clock next morning. All in all, it was a very good afternoon's work. And it meant that his phone was engaged almost non-stop. Any other parent who wanted to get through to him would have to wait until next morning, and by then his counter-measures should have begun to make their effect. He was pleased with himself. It would not even have bothered him greatly if he had known that several times during the afternoon's work Inspector Pumfrey had listened in on his extension in the study.

As his spiel developed into a formula, smoothly and convincingly delivered, Septimus Coffin allowed his mind to wander a little. Allowed it, for example, to speculate on whom he would most like to be arrested for the murder of Hilary Frome. Without malice he did it, but do it he did. Percy Makepeace, he finally decided. With Muggeridge a good second. And Corbett Farraday an also-ran, pleasant though he was in a hamsterish kind of way. These three were more than just expendable: the school would be better for their departure. So it would be, too, for the departure of Iain McWhirter, but he was, alas, not expendable from a financial point of view.

Coffin meditated, too, on the long-term future. Would it be possible, he wondered, to persuade Miss Gilberd to move with her mother into the headmaster's quarters and take general charge of the boarding section? She would be very good at it. Motherly in the best and most no-nonsense meaning of the term. He himself had no desire to shift the possessions of a lifetime, or to live on the job and have boys after school as well as during it. He wondered whether to sack Mrs Garfitt on the spot, but decided to give her leave for a few days, and bring his sister in to manage the institution's food. Mrs Garfitt's sense of economy had no doubt been carried too far under the enthusiastic prodding of Enid Crumwallis, but no private school in the current financial climate could afford to sneeze at the ability to haggle, scent out a bargain or simply cheat. And those abilities Mrs Garfitt possessed in abundance.

So, all in all, it was a satisfying, fulfilling afternoon. Now all that was required was a speedy arrest, and the right arrest. It was all very well building castles in the air, but would Percy Makepeace make a convincing murderer? Would anyone, he wondered, believe that he had the *nerve*?

'No, Mr Muggeridge,' said Superintendent Pumfrey firmly. 'I'm quite sure Mr Freely can take the football game. I don't want our talk interrupted any further.'

Bill Muggeridge took it with the sort of philosophy always shown by someone who has a Hardyesque feeling that in this life nothing much good is ever going to happen to *them*. He ambled into the study again, and sat down, muttering. It was not surprising he had wished to put off the evil hour, for Mike Pumfrey's temper had very clearly not been improved by the interruption. His toothbrush moustache, indeed, seemed to bristle and assume a life of its own, independent of the flesh beneath. The case, to him, was beginning to bear all the hallmarks of the work of a madman: it had the madman's simplicity of means, the madman's daring, the madman's wholesale and indiscriminate bloodthirstiness. Pumfrey had found the deadly sliver of glass on the floor of the dining hall, with fragments of shepherd's pie still clinging to it. If it had gone further down the throat of the boy to whose lot it fell, it could certainly have killed him. Pumfrey's temper had not been improved by the hysteria of Mrs Garfitt, which he suspected of being a mixture of concern for herself and her job, and sheer amateur dramatics. Mrs Crumwallis had topped off his disgust with the case, the school and the personnel involved by her reaction to his order that no more of the pie be served or eaten.

'But the waste!' she had said, not knowing that the financial position of the school was no longer her affair.

'By gum!' Pumfrey had muttered through his teeth, resolving to save himself till later, as far as Enid Crumwallis was concerned.

So he was brusque to the point of intimidation when, at last, he had Bill Muggeridge in front of him again. He leant forward, fixed him with his cold blue eyes, twitched his moustache, and made it clear that there was to be no more nonsense.

'Right—this time let's have the truth, and no shilly-shallying or silly-buggering around. Why did you think your wife was going out to meet Hilary Frome?'

'Well, I'd seen them, hadn't I?' said Bill, shoving his chin forward suggestively, as if he were arguing with the ref. 'Seen them together. Monday, it was, or Tuesday, I forget, but they met up by the trees, the ones separating the headmaster's lawn from the football pitch.'

'I see. And you were nearby and saw them?'

'I was refereeing a game, wasn't I?' said Bill, who seemed to have slipped into an interrogative rut. 'All the kids saw them as well. Bloody embarrassing. Not that they know her ways like I do, but boys of that age will snigger at anything.'

'Her ways?'

'Her little come-hither methods. Looking up, with her head tilted to one side. Brushing against him with her thigh. I've seen it often enough. Fell for it myself, come to that. Gawd—it makes me puke.'

'How old is your wife, Mr Muggeridge?'

'Hell, I don't know—twenty-nine? Thirty?'

'Wasn't Hilary Frome a bit—?'

'Young? She's not against baby-snatching, if she fancies the baby. Mind you, she normally goes for more mature men, I grant you. But probably going with someone as young as that would—I dunno—act as a sort of tonic—know what I mean? A pick-me-up. Convince her she wasn't over the hump, if you get me.'

'Oh, I get you. Now, you decided to follow them. What exactly were you after?'

'After?' Bill scratched his head, and Pumfrey sensed the beginnings of prevarication. 'I dunno. I hadn't really worked it out.' And that was certainly possible. Bill Muggeridge generally had the air of a man whose motives were a muddle, whose plans of action were anything but carefully calculated modes of procedure.

'I wanted to catch them,' he said, finally.

'Was it jealousy?'

'Blimey, no. Bit late in the day for that.'

'Was it really fear you'd lose your job?'

'Well, partly. And then, if it was with little golden-haired boy Hilary Frome, it would give me a marvellous lever with old Crumwallis. Then, you see, Onyx and me, we're pretty much washed up as it is, and I did wonder . . .'

'Yes?'

'Well, there's all those kids . . . not mine, most of them . . . and she'd screw me for maintenance, get every penny she could . . . And I thought to myself, judges don't like that sort of thing . . .'

'What sort of thing?'

'Older women having it off with boys. It's even worse than *vice versa*. They put on their specs and lay about them with words like "degenerate" and "sick" — lay it on real nasty. Now I'm going to need a judge on my side when it comes to maintenance for those little bastards of hers, so I thought it would help if I could prove that that's what she's been up to. If it ever came to that, of course . . .'

Pumfrey had cooled down during Bill Muggeridge's muddled dissection of his own grubby motives, for the contemplation of the murkier side of the human race must always have a grain of fascination to a policeman. Now a flash of inspiration showed him a further layer to Bill Muggeridge's unsavoury motivation.

'Ah!' he said. 'You thought it wouldn't come to that?'

Bill Muggeridge looked mighty cunning.

'Well, I did wonder. The Fromes are pretty big around here. Pots of money. Must have— all these doctors have. And Hilary being the Great White Hope, the coming Frome, and all that . . .'

'You thought they'd buy you off?'

'Well, if you want to put it like that. Perhaps a lump sum. Or maybe they'd be willing to help with Onyx's brats if Hilary was kept out of it. I was damn sure they wouldn't want Hilary's future spoilt, his name bandied about. I mean, I hadn't worked it out . . .'

'You were tossing several balls in the air?'

'That's it. More or less.'

'The trouble was, you never caught them.'

'What? Oh, *them*. No, I didn't, and that was that. The story of my life: the big chance, and then — poof — it goes up in smoke as I watch. I could have made a nice little thing for myself there, one way or another.'

'Hmmm. Do you think they did, in fact, get together?'

'Well, I *thought* they did. Last night. But listening to the boys, it sounds as if that bugger Frome stayed in the boarding annexe all evening. So I dunno. Might suit his nasty sense of humour to lead her on and then stand her up.'

'It might, at that. What does your wife say?'

'Says she just went for a walk. Stupid cow. You don't put a ring round the date two days ahead to remind yourself you're going for a walk.'

'No. Well, I may have to talk to your wife —'

'Best of British to you.'

'And when, by the way, did you get home?'

'Get home? Well, it was just after the end of *Coronation Street*. The eldest kid was watching.'

'Say eight-five. And did you go into the school or the boarding annexe?'

'No, 'course I didn't. They wouldn't have gone in there. I looked around the grounds, on the playing fields.'

'And the bird, or birds, had flown. I see. Well, I'm sorry your enterprise came to nothing —'

'Oh, that —'

'You seem to have had a nice little scheme worked out there.'

'Well —'

'Could well have brought you in a few quid one way or another.'

'That's what I —'

'I don't think I'll be wanting you again for a bit. Oh, and Mr Muggeridge —'

'Yes?'

'You strike me as one of the grimiest individuals I've met for many a long day, and I assure you I do meet 'em. Close the door behind you on the way out, won't you?'

Bill Muggeridge, stunned into even greater inarticulacy than usual, shuffled out and shut the door. Mike Pumfrey, who had enjoyed orchestrating the little litany of the last minutes of the interview, watched him with a smile on his face, then he banged his pencil down on the desk.

'Manure,' he said.

'Oh, I don't know,' said the more generous Fenniway.

'Oh, you liked him, did you? He struck you as a prepossessing specimen of your average, likeable human being?'

'Give over,' said Fenniway, who was accustomed to his boss's use of his occasional bursts of articulateness. 'But still, he's fairly human. Grubby, so to speak, but not evil.'

'And therefore not a murderer, you'd say?'

'That's what I was thinking.'

'I'm not so sure. Some murderers I've met have been far from flaming brands of wickedness. Remember Margaret Hicks? No, she was probably before your time. Pushed her grandma over the cliffs when she thought no one was looking, just for the contents of her handbag. She wasn't evil. The judge said so. He practically apologized for having to send her to prison, the way some of them do these days. She was a bit like this Muggeridge: a grubby little soul. That sort does the first thing that comes into their heads, because there's nothing inside there that tells them not to. That's what laws are for—to persuade them not to do it.'

'Well—maybe. But this doesn't look like a murder done on impulse, sir.'

'No, agreed. But I wish I had a better idea of what it did look like. At the moment it looks like the murderous pranks of a maniac with a hatred of kids, but—'

He was interrupted by the ring of the telephone.

'Yes?' said Pumfrey, grabbing it. 'Oh—you've got them. Right. Some solution of aconite? Well, it figures. Thought it could be something of the kind . . . No. Say that again . . . It was *what*? No, I sure as hell didn't. No . . . No. Well, ring back if anything else comes in.'

He banged down the phone and looked at Fenniway.

'Well, sir?'

'Well, Sergeant. It seems we've been damned fools. It seems we've been barking up the wrong tree. The poison was in the medicine glass.'

'*What?*'

'Precisely. And in the medicine. It had been doctored while it sat outside the sick bay, I suppose. Or perhaps . . .'

'But that means—?'

'Precisely. Now we know why Pickerage was so scared. And now we're bloody back to square one.'

CHAPTER 13

TURNABOUT

The Burleigh School was haunted that afternoon. The navy blue ghost of Mr Crumwallis flitted dispiritedly around the rooms and corridors that once had formed his domain. It was a peering, watery-eyed ghost, one that cleared its throat and let its hand flutter to its mouth in ineffectual gestures. Perhaps Mr Crumwallis was looking his last on the symbols of his state, a Balkan monarch taking a last look round his shoddy nineteenth-century palace before the new regime shunted him off by train to pathetic exile in Baden-Baden or Estoril. Perhaps he was meditating some fantastic turn of events that could restore him to power and prestige. Perhaps he was meditating revenge. He wandered miserably from his private kitchen through the hall, and then down the corridors—being careful not to be seen—that housed the classrooms. He wandered over the lawn and let himself in to the boarding annexe, but seeing a last stray police constable at the top of the stairs he hrrumphed, stammered a word of excuse and shuffled back to his own quarters.

In his private hall—his, though, no longer—he paused, pretending to admire the watercolour of Dedham High Street, painted by the maiden aunt of one of the school's headmasters in the 'thirties. From here he could hear the voice of Septimus Coffin, on the 'phone in his sitting-room. What was he saying? What was he saying about *him?* How deceived he had been in that man, that elderly cast-off from the Cullbridge Grammar School. He had nursed a viper in his double-breasted. Coffin had revealed himself a man fit for treasons, stratagems and . . . whatever else the poet had said. Spoils, that was it. Spoils. How very apt.

He wandered over to the other side of the hall, where a tentative oil by the same amateur artist showed Flatford Mill and a dismal inability to master the new medium. He was by the study door, but he could hear almost nothing. The study had been effectively soundproofed, perhaps by some predecessor addicted to flagellation. No sound emerged from it. But he knew that the Superintendent was interviewing his wife. His Enid. The partner of his labours. Stupid cow.

In that estimate, for once, Mr Crumwallis was at one with the Superintendent. Mike Pumfrey had by now spent some time battling at the pebbly surface of Enid Crumwallis's complacency, and he had got nowhere. Others, subjected to Pumfrey's inquisitorial brusqueness, became shrill or hysterical in their self-justifications. Not so Enid Crumwallis. She was convinced not only that she had acted with impeccable logic and discretion, but also that all right-thinking people would have done precisely the same. Like many stupid people, she identified her stupidity with common sense.

'Of course I didn't leave it in his room,' she said with grim composure. 'The boy might have thought that the more he had, the quicker he'd get well. He might have developed a taste for it.'

'Hardly likely,' began Mike Pumfrey.

'I don't know about that.' She leaned forward, as if imparting a fascinating secret. 'Did you know some of them sniff glue bottles and burn banana skins? Doesn't bear thinking about. If they can do that, they can do anything.'

And she leant back once more in her chair and tightened her lips at the thought of the limitless depravity of adolescence.

'The point I am trying to make,' said Pumfrey, without any notable display of patience, 'is that medicine should be locked up.'

'Oh, well, medicine,' said Enid Crumwallis.

'You don't count this as medicine?'

'Of course, it *is* genuine,' she said, 'but still . . .'

'Some of the things you give them are *not* genuine, then?'

'Cold tea and aniseed!' said Mrs Crumwallis, with a palpable air of triumph. "I put it in old bottles. Mostly these boys are just putting it on, you know, or just imagining things. The cold tea does as good as anything, and the aniseed makes it taste nasty, as they expect. It's well known people take too much medicine. Did you know that when doctors go on strike the death rate always goes down? People these days are just soft, running along for a packet of pills every time they think they've got an ache. I once thought I'd go in for Christian Science, but I couldn't find the time . . .'

'I see,' said Pumfrey, his sharp little eyes glistening.

'And do your medical theories also contenance giving a boy a stomach medicine when he is running a fever?'

'Same thing,' said Enid Crumwallis gnomically.

'Hmmm,' said Pumfrey. 'Well, I suppose he ought to be grateful you didn't pull one of his teeth out. Well now, you left the medicine — you say this was genuine? —'

'Oh yes. I get it wholesale.'

' — you left it outside the sick bay, in the corridor. How long had it been there?'

'Since he had his last lot. That was about three.'

'Anybody could have got at it, then?'

'Any of the boys could have.'

'Anybody else?'

'*I* don't know, do I? Not my business to go round finding out where all the staff are every minute of the day. There wouldn't be anybody much about between three and quarter to four. That's when school ends. Pickerage would be the only one around in the boarding annexe before then.'

Except, Pumfrey thought, if someone had had the last period free. He made a mental note to check.

'And after school ended?'

'Oh well, after that they're all milling around, all the boarders, that is. Having their tea and whatnot. Noisy little brats. Later on most of them went out on the lawn. Supposedly practising cricket with that Frome boy.'

'I know,' said Pumfrey. His moustache bristled involuntarily as he noticed the decided lack of compassion in her tone for one who had after all breathed his last in her lap.

'Anyone could have gone up while they were out there,' pursued Mrs Crumwallis.

'I see,' said Mike. 'Tell me, did you have the same high opinion of Hilary Frome as your husband, Mrs Crumwallis?'

'Oh, *him*,' said the headmaster's wife, and then went

silent, so that Mike Pumfrey was unsure whether her contempt was directed at her husband, or at his star pupil. Eventually she resumed: 'I don't go much on boys. Dark ones, fair ones, fat ones, thin ones, to me they're no different, the one from the other. Nasty little imps, every one of them, and if you started having favourites, they'd put it over you, sure as God made apples. If I liked boys I couldn't do my job.'

'Which is?'

'To run this school so it makes a profit. We're not in this business for charity, you know.'

'No. I can see that. I'm not sure you're in it for education either.'

'Oh really? Well, I'd have you know there's plenty who are grateful to have a school like this in the town.'

'I'm sure you're right. But as far as I'm concerned, Mrs Crumwallis, I'd rather send a kid of mine to the nearest Borstal than put him here under your care. I'd say the sooner you get out of this business into some other, the better it will be. Good morning to you.'

Mrs Crumwallis stared at him. She blinked, as she imprinted an impression of him on a card in her mental filing cabinet, stored under the heading 'impertinence'. Then she rose from her chair, and peered down at him again from her great height. Then she did a right about turn and marched to the door. But as she opened it she turned around, and as a parting shot said:

'Hoity-toity!'

And she closed the door with a bang.

Fenniway thought Mike Pumfrey was going to explode. He certainly had to repress the desire to spring over to the door, fling it open and bellow at her some crushing obscenity, so as to get the final word. But suddenly, instead, he relaxed in a great shout of laughter.

'Well,' he said, finally. 'I'm certainly hearing new things today. I never expected to hear anyone say "hoity-toity" at me while I was going about my official business. That's what comes of having a different kind of customer to deal with.'

'Bit of a character,' remarked Fenniway neutrally.

'Bit of a tartar, too. My God—what a dried-up old stick. No wonder the headmaster gets sentimental crushes on fair-haired cricketers.'

'And that's not the worst of her,' said Fenniway.

'No, not by a long chalk. Negligent, mean-minded, and very, very stupid . . . You know, Fenniway, I wish we could get back to our old ideas: someone getting at Hilary Frome, or perhaps someone getting at the headmaster and his lovely lady wife. It figured, it came together. Someone getting at Pickerage is so much less likely. But I really don't see . . .'

'I did wonder,' said Fenniway, 'if possibly the evidence could have been tampered with afterwards.'

Pumfrey meditated.

'Before we arrived, you mean? It's a thought. There was chaos over there. The glasses could have been rinsed, and poison put in the medicine, instead . . . But no, that's nonsense. What would be the point? Who would go to that trouble, take the risk? Because they would have had to wash out the sherry bottle and put clean sherry back . . . If it were that, it would narrow it down to the boys and the Crumwallises . . . But it's no good trying to fit theories to fact. What we've got to build on is that the poison was in the medicine and in the medicine glass. So either they were out for Pickerage, or—' he sighed—'the medicine was poisoned much earlier, and by someone who just didn't care a damn who they killed. The same person who put that glass into the shepherd's pie. My God, Fenniway, I wish I could be sure if we're looking for a maniac, or for someone who's taken advantage of a maniac's doings.'

'I suppose we'd better see Pickerage again, hadn't we?'

'Oh yes. We'll have to get it confirmed, get it all down

on paper. Can't say I'm looking forward to it.'

'But he realizes already, don't you think, sir? That's what he's been afraid of all along.'

'Oh yes—bound to be. But why the hell didn't he say something to us, when he talked to us last night?'

'I've been thinking about that, sir. From what we can gather, from young Freely, for example, this Pickerage could have been something in the nature of Frome's second-in-command, wouldn't you say?'

'Could well be. In other words, he himself might have quite a lot to hide, you mean?'

'Yes, sir. And also might equally be open to attack. If Frome was hated, Pickerage might be too.'

Mike Pumfrey's sharp little face was twisted into a grimace.

'Might be. But from the little I know about kids, it's hard to imagine. This Pickerage seems such a different type, that you've got to admit. And a fairly likeable type, even if he might be pretty aggravating to have in a class. Oh well, you'd better get him in. Where is he?'

'Still locked in upstairs. Oh—he's all right: he ate his meal, and he's over with the fever. But Walls, the constable upstairs, says he mashed up the pie and inspected every mouthful. So he's still feeling pretty threatened.'

'He will be, till we've got to the bottom of this. Will you go and get him?'

Out in the hallway Sergeant Fenniway spotted the dejected shades of Mr and Mrs Crumwallis, deep in converse. The shades melted through the door of their private kitchen when they spotted him. When he came back with Pickerage, Pumfrey thought the boy looked very much healthier than he had last night, though not a great deal happier.

'Sit down there, Malcolm—is that the name?' said Pumfrey, trying to be a little less brusque this time. 'Right, now I'm not going to beat about the bush. I want the whole truth from you this time.'

Some reflex action operated in Pickerage, some reflex action born of innumerable collisions with teachers and heads, interviews where he was accused of something or other that he had indeed done. He put on a look of seraphic innocence. He became the little boy in *Jane Eyre* who assured Mr Brocklehurst that he preferred learning psalms to being given ginger nuts.

'But I told you the whole truth yesterday.'

'No, you didn't, Malcolm. You told us some, but you missed out a bit. I want to know what happened between Hilary Frome pouring your medicine and the two of you toasting each other—"your health", was it?—and drinking up.'

Pickerage's eyes had dropped. He swallowed hard.

'He . . . there was a lot of noise from the dorm . . . and he . . . Hilary, he went over to the door and shouted at them to shut up.'

He faded into silence.

'And you?'

'I . . . changed the glasses.' He looked up, his eyes filled with tears, his voice going to stratospheric heights. 'It was just a joke. I didn't know. I mean, how could I? And they were both brown, you see—the sherry and old Mother C.'s filthy stuff. And I thought . . . I thought it would be a good laugh.'

'Yes. We see that. We understand. We knew that was what must have happened when we found out that the poison was in the glass with medicine in. Was this why you were so upset yesterday night, when you talked to us?'

Pickerage's eyes had dropped again.

'Well . . . yes. I mean it was like I'd killed Hilary, wasn't it? And he was my friend. I'd poisoned him.'

'No, you mustn't think that, Malcolm. You hadn't poisoned him because you didn't know there was poison in the medicine, did you?'

'No-o . . .'

'There's something else worrying you, isn't there?'

Pickerage raised his eyes and looked straight at him.

'Of course there is. Don't be daft. If somebody put stuff in that medicine, they were trying to poison *me*.'

'Well,' said Pumfrey, 'maybe.' He shifted uncomfortably in his chair. There was no way of being cosy and matey with the boy in this sort of conversation. 'And does that mean you can think of some reason why anybody should want to poison you?'

Pickerage looked aggrieved.

' 'Course I can't. Mind you, I've thought about it. Tried to puzzle it out. I mean, I know old Stinko doesn't like me—'

'Old Stinko? Is that the science teacher?'

'No-o-o,' said Pickerage contemptuously. 'It's Muggeridge. He pongs worse than the bogs sometimes. I told you, he gets downs on people. But, I mean, *poison*. He wouldn't . . . would he?'

'No. No, of course he wouldn't. Are you sure there's no one else who disliked you?'

'No. Why should they dislike me? I mean, the head slippers me, and that, but that's *different*, isn't it?'

'Of course it is. Now, you and Hilary Frome were friends, weren't you?'

'Yes, we were. He was my best friend.'

'And a lot of people disliked Hilary Frome, didn't they?'

Pickerage thought.

'Well, I suppose so. I suppose the staff and that disliked him. I mean, he ragged them. Said things . . . You see, he thought this place was the *end*.'

'So I gather. Malcolm, what did you and Hilary Frome do on Sunday?'

The suddenness of the question caught Pickerage out, and a great blush burst out over his boyish face.

'We . . . we went out.'

'Yes . . .'

'We went out for the day.'

'Where did you go?'

'We went to Stanhope Woods. There's not many people go there, even on Sunday.'

'Yes. And what did you do?'

'We just talked.'

'Why did you want to go where there wouldn't be anybody around if all you wanted to do was to talk?'

'Well . . . well, we had things to talk about.'

'Come off it, Malcolm. You don't blush about a bit of talk. What did you do? I'm not the headmaster. What was it?'

Pickerage's face looked like sunset over the Alps. He stared down into his lap.

'We did something . . . something Hilary wanted to do. It was nasty. He said I'd like it, but I didn't . . . It hurt.'

'I see. You're not the first to have done that, old boy, you know. But perhaps you'd better tell me exactly what—'

But Pickerage was saved from further embarrassment. The door of the study was flung open, and a splendid and costly vision, in fur cape and Givenchy suit, waltzed into the room, wafting in her wake a breath of spring on the Champs-Elysées, captured just for her, and bottled and retailed at a ridiculous price. She smiled a wide smile, of wonder and self-satisfaction at her own loveliness and desirability.

'Malcolm! Darling! They said I'd find you here. *Not* in trouble again, surely, darling? And you—' she turned the full force of her abundant sexual appeal on Mr Pumfrey—'you must be the new headmaster!'

CHAPTER 14

MOTHERS

It was the first time, in all the visits she had paid to Burleigh School, that Malcolm Pickerage had been pleased to see his mother.

The same could not be said of Superintendent Pumfrey.

'No,' he rapped out. 'I am not the new headmaster.'

'Really?' she said, with a sweet, soft, inquiring smile. She came over to the desk, and Pumfrey was overwhelmingly conscious of scent, of a soft, clinging material, something between corn and orange in shade, and of the smile, now invitingly close and (as they say about duplicated letters that look convincing) personalized. As an afterthought, she put her hand on Pickerage's shoulder, fondly.

'Seeing you there, behind the desk, I naturally thought . . .' she went on. 'One of the boys outside, you see, told me that the school *had* a new headmaster . . .'

'Yes. I believe that is so. It's not my concern, but I understand Mr. Coffin has taken over.'

'Oh, but I *know* him. I've met him. Quite old, but definitely sympathetic, wouldn't you say? Someone one could have complete *trust* in? I don't think *personally* that I'll miss Mr Crumwallis, you know. I expect some people were impressed, and possibly he *was* some kind of scholar, but I must say I expect myself a more *manly* man at the head of a boys' school. If you see what I mean.'

She opened her eyes wide at him, to tell him that he would precisely fit the bill. Mike Pumfrey wondered what sort of man there still was around who responded to such outrageously outdated appeals. Elderly businessmen, he would guess. Huffing slightly, he turned his head towards her son.

'Malcolm, perhaps you'd better run along now. I expect you'd like to go out with your mother later, wouldn't you? Have a meal, or something?'

"Oh—a meal,' put in his mother. 'I don't know if I—'

'Yes. Super,' said Pickerage, the parody schoolboy. 'I'll go and get changed.'

Once he had gone, his mother sat somewhat stiffly in his chair, fixed Mike Pumfrey again with those liquid eyes that were definitely now less inviting, and said:

'Just what *is* this all about?'

Mike Pumfrey cleared his throat.

'I'm sorry if I committed you there, but your son has gone through a pretty terrible time, Mrs Pickerage, and—'

He had trodden, inadvertently, on a button that produced an automatic response.

'Oh, darling, *please* not that. I haven't been that for many years. I'm Veronica Furley. I reverted to my maiden name. My friends call me Ronny.'

Sergeant Fenniway, awake to the sign, noticed that his superior's moustache gave a totally spontaneous, and eloquent, bristle. Privately Mike Pumfrey was thinking that Veronica Furley was really too 'twenties for words.

'Well, Miss Furley,' he began, hardly able to resist the temptation to call her Ms, 'I'm a police officer.'

'I knew it! I wouldn't want you to think I've often been involved, but I felt sure I knew the signs. *What* on earth has been going on?'

So Mike Pumfrey launched into an explanation. He made it as unsensational as possible, but the bare facts were striking enough. Veronica Furley, though she put up almost no pretence of any motherly concern, seemed to listen with a most commendable appetite for the sensational. She let him continue uninterrupted until the end.

'Well, I *say!* Poor old Malcolm. Practically did the blighter in himself, didn't he?'

'No. *No*, Miss Furley. It was totally inadvertent. Please don't say anything like that to *him*.'

'But of *course* not. Though I think I'd be horribly excited. But you think somebody may have been trying to get at him, do you?'

'It's an obvious possibility—something we have to investigate, at any rate.'

'*What* a little beast he must have been. Of course he's a dead bore quite a lot of the time, but I wouldn't have thought . . . *Damn!* I suppose this means I'll have to look round for another school for him.'

'He certainly seems to want to go somewhere else. At the moment, anyway. But I wouldn't be in too much of a hurry, if I were you. We may have this cleared up in no time, and then he could well change his mind.'

'Still, I *have* been thinking of it. I mean, people *ask* me, people who know about him, and of course The Burleigh School cuts no ice, no ice at all. I always tell them it's because the boarding section is so small, though of course I realize the boarding section is so small because the school is no good. I say it's like being part of a big family, but then I think of that bony woman with the specs, and practically burst out laughing. I mean, she is too workhouse for words, don't you think?'

'Certainly I'd think twice if it were my own.'

'Would you? Too sweet. Of course I value your opinion e*nor*mously. And now there *is* some money, it would be possible. Perhaps I'd better take him out to dinner, then I can tell him I'll look for somewhere with just a tiny bit of prestige. God knows, he's no brain, so he'll need any old school network that might be going if he's going to make anything of himself.'

'Well, you could discuss it,' said Mike Pumfrey, knowing very well the congenital disinclination of children to change schools, and thinking Pickerage had had enough material for traumas for one day. 'If I were you I'd let him make the final decision.'

She looked at him as if the idea of children having the right to any opinion on their own future seemed to her quirky in the extreme. Then she smiled her soft, feminine smile.

'I expect he'll do as I say,' she said. 'But you *must* tell me more about the Crumwallises. You never know, this may hit the headlines. *So* thrilling to be in the thick of it. Do people think he did it? Is that why they got the boot?'

'We've no reason to suspect Mr Crumwallis,' said Pumfrey severely. 'The internal affairs of the school are no concern of ours, but I don't think it's quite accurate to say he got the boot. I gather parents got anxious when rumours started going around about the medicine. There were doubts about Mrs Crumwallis's competence in general. There was a danger of the school folding up altogether, and Mr Crumwallis snatched at the best offer for the school he could get.'

'Really? Is that all? Parents are so silly and protective, aren't they? Not that it's not *appalling* to think that Malcolm might have drunk that stuff . . . But you know, there *might* be something else there. Malcolm told me about this Frome last time I was here. Couldn't stop talking about him, you know what children are like. I've forgotten most of it, if I ever really listened, but he did I'm sure say he was the apple of the headmaster's eye, and all that. Did you say he was a handsome boy?'

'I didn't, but yes: I think most people would say he was that.'

'Well, there you are. They'd probably had a fumble, or worse, and the boy was blackmailing him. They're so *up* in things these days, aren't they? I suppose it must be the television. But then, there's so *much* of it around, isn't there, they're bound to hear things. I heard that *fearsome* Miss Grower lost her job for something of the kind. Terrifies me, darling, really she does! Not *that*, of course, but that *look* she gives me every time we meet, that just *shows* she thinks me a social butterfly or something of the kind!'

She smiled, and fluttered her wings, or her eyelashes.

'You say Malcolm told you about Hilary Frome. Could you remember anything he told you, I wonder?'

'Oh, darling—that is asking a lot. I mean, a boy talking about another boy! I didn't even realize the boy was fifteen, and even if I had . . . *Not* my weakness, I assure you . . . No, he just burbled on about him, you know, in the way kids do, and it did occur to me to *wonder*, if you know what I mean. But that kind's usually been horribly mothered, haven't they, and I assure you that's one thing Malcolm simply *can't* accuse me of. Oh, he talked about this and that—mostly about jokes this boy had played on the teachers, and things he'd said to them. All that *Tom Brown* stuff isn't really to my taste, as you can imagine. To tell you the truth—I wouldn't admit this to everyone—having a boy Malcolm's age is *really* a bit of an embarrassment.'

She said it in an outburst of candour, apparently expecting it to come as a revelation. Mike Pumfrey sighed.

'I see, well—'

'There! I can see I've taken up *much* too much of your time,' said Veronica Furley, standing up, and fixing him with a look of crushing intimacy. 'I'd better collect the little brute and take him off somewhere. *Where* on earth, I ask you, does one take a thirteen-year-old boy to dinner? In Cullbridge, too. And if I drive out to one of these *madly* expensive little country places, it would be sure to be full to the brim with people I know. It happens all the time when I'm with . . . Oh well—*so* pleased to have met you, Mr—'

'Miss . . . er . . . Furley—' said Mike Pumfrey, standing up in his turn but furrowing his brow, knowing that something had got past him in the foregoing chatter, but not sure what it was. 'There was something else. Something you said I meant to ask you about . . . Oh, yes. Money. You said, when you were talking about schools for Malcolm, that there was more money now.'

Veronica Furley sat down again, gracefully but determined. Pumfrey wondered whether he had been wise to ask, because it was clear this was a subject bitterly close to her heart, and he wondered whether he would ever be able to get her out of the study. There was an expression of long-suppressed grievance on her lovely, soap-advertisement face.

'Well, of course there is, *now*. When I think how much I needed it when I *first* sent Malcolm here, and how I *tried* to screw more out of his father, and not a penny did I get without *running* to lawyers every week of my life. And now . . .'

'Yes?'

'Well, now: there it is. Not mine, though, more's the pity. And *really*, I'd have thought it *should* have been. He was my father, after all. He died about six months ago. You may have read about it in the papers. A *release*, a blessed release. Not for him, it was quite sudden, but for me. Well, he was in agriculture, you know, very big: he'd been high up in the National Farmers' Union, that's why it was in all the papers. You wouldn't think I was practically *born* in Wellington boots, would you? Anyway, most of it went to my brother, who runs the businesses—farms and orchards and things—but he left forty thousand to Malcolm. *In trust*, I may say. That did rather hurt me, I admit. Of course, he and Malcolm had always got on like a house on fire. That's where he went mostly in the holidays. But I mean — his lawyer and my brother are the trustees. I thought that a bit of cheek, not including me. Though I admit that money *does* have a habit of running through my fingers, quite remarkably quickly sometimes. But the fact is, I'm expected to *crawl* to the trustees every time I want the smallest little thing for Malcolm. I have thought of sending them every single bill, for socks and vests, the lot. But anyway, in this case, if it was a matter of Malcolm's education, I imagine they could hardly refuse, do you?'

'Probably not,' admitted Pumfrey. 'If that's what the boy wants. So if things go according to plan, your son will come into a fair income when he is — what — twenty-one?'

'That's right. If only Daddy had made it eighteen I might have hoped to wangle something out of him, but he'll probably be *frightfully* adult at twenty-one, and *cling* to it like grim death.'

'And if he were to die?'

'The money? Oh heavens, I don't know. You don't think it could be poor little me, do you? But I *don't* think so, Superintendent, so *please* don't start putting me down as an unnatural mother who slips poison into her own child's drink, like that awful woman Sian Phillips played in the television series about Rome or wherever it was. I should think it just gets distributed among the other grandchildren, or goes back into the estate, or something. I tell you, Daddy and I simply didn't get on. He thought me — you can't imagine — flighty! Ah well. Goodbye, *dear* Mr Pumfrey. You *will* keep me posted, won't you. I shall be *waiting* for a call — positively on tenterhooks!'

And she waltzed out of the room to undertake the heavy duty of taking her son out to dinner.

'Stupid bitch!' said Pumfrey. 'Stupid, made-up, pretentious, shallow bitch.'

'Quite a dish, though,' said Sergeant Fenniway.

'I hate her type,' said Pumfrey, entirely unnecessarily.

'I'd like to think she might have slipped into the annexe and done it, but she would hardly have come along volunteering that information about the money if that's what she'd been occupying her spare time with. But money there is: another piece towards the puzzle. Why do people always compare an investigation to a jigsaw puzzle, Fenniway? Half the pieces don't fit into the picture because they're totally irrelevant. This may well be one of them. But still, it's a solid motive — for someone.'

'Makes a change, anyway,' said Fenniway, who liked his killings clear-cut, and usually got them just that.

'Precisely. A change from the option of a series of pranks — dangerous and nasty ones, some of them — leading up to the biggest prank of all, a murder.'

'Or alternatively a series of pranks which someone takes advantage of, so that the murder looks like part of a series.'

'Exactly. Or, now, a third possibility: that there is no connection between the two, and the murder was an attempt by someone outside the school to kill Pickerage — someone who had no knowledge of what had been going on here. There's something to be said for the third option: as you said, it's the first solid motive, though forty thou' is by no means so solid a motive as it would have been ten or fifteen years ago.'

'Still, even today, forty thou', coming at the right time,' began Sergeant Fenniway, for whom now would certainly be the right time for forty thousand to come. He could well have waxed lyrical on the subject, being a prospective father and a would-be house-buyer, but he was interrupted by a knock at the door.

'Come in,' roared Pumfrey, in his most fearsome voice. He feared it might be Mr Crumwallis, come for further heart-searching, or perhaps to unburden his soul on the loss of his school, and he was getting into a suitably off-putting mood. But the head that poked itself round the door turned out to be Penny Warlock's, and she did not appear to be intimidated.

'Hello,' she said. 'I'm sorry to bother you, but I saw that awful woman swanning it down the drive with poor Malcolm, and I thought you might be free.'

'Come in, come in,' said Pumfrey, with a sudden switch to genuine geniality. He thought how attractive, how very attractive Penny was, and what a refreshing, common-sense change after his last encounter. Sergeant Fenniway, too, looked as if his thoughts had easily been diverted from his insubstantial forty thousand.

'Come in and sit down,' said Mike. 'I suppose you've remembered something you ought to have told us?'

'No,' said Penny, staying by the door. 'It's nothing to do with me, at all.' She darted a look into the hall, then shut the door and came over to the desk. 'It's this girl. I found her outside, wandering about in the drive, when I slipped out for a breath of air. I found I couldn't bear any more Hilary Frome in the Common Room, and I went out the front door and there she was—'

'Who?'

'She *says* she's Hilary Frome's girlfriend. She says she's looking for you. For the policeman investigating his murder. She doesn't seem to have anything special to tell you, as far as I can make out, but she just wants to talk to you. And she is in a terrible state. Of course she has no business to be in the school grounds at all, so I spirited her in here, which is really private quarters. Do you think you could see her?'

'Oh God,' said Pumfrey. 'I suppose I'd better.'

'You will be gentle with her, won't you?' said Penny. 'She's very upset.'

'I do have girls of my own, Miss Warlock,' said Mike Pumfrey in a tired voice, as if he'd never bullied anyone in the entire course of his police career.

'Oh — of course. Sorry,' said Penny, and she backed out of the room.

But when she had bundled her charge into the room (and darted away thankfully herself), Pumfrey could see that she had certainly not exaggerated about the girl's being upset. It was difficult to imagine a more pathetic bundle of teenage misery than the one standing by the door: her face was streaked by salt tears and dirt, her hair was in rats' tails around her oval face, her skirt was dirty and damp, perhaps from her collapsing to the ground in despair. A steady rhythm of sobs racked her body, and when they lurched convulsively out into the open she dabbed at her face with a sodden handkerchief. Only when, now and then, she straightened her shoulders to let a violent burst emerge did the two men notice that she was well-formed, had the beginnings of a fine figure. Thinking back to their own schooldays, they could imagine that in adolescent circles she might well have been a catch, and perhaps also a tease.

Pumfrey took from an inside pocket an enormous clean white handkerchief, and gestured to her with it.

'Here. Have this. Come and sit down.' The girl let out a howl, as if she were being shown Hilary Frome's shroud. But she came over, took the handkerchief, and made some more effective efforts to dam the flood and repair the damage to her face. Finally she sank down into a chair.

'That's better. You wanted to see me, you know, so you've got to get yourself in hand if you want to have a talk. You're Margaret Wilkinson, aren't you?'

She opened her eyes with shock, and suddenly the sobs stopped.

'How did you know?'

'Oh, your name has come up. In the course of conversation. You're Hilary Frome's girlfriend, aren't you?'

'I was!' A single sob, almost a cry, escaped her.

'Oh—you mean it was over?'

'No! I mean that he's dead!' She dabbed at her face, but then she looked up at Pumfrey, and he saw how beautiful she one day would be: almond-shaped face, beautifully-moulded eyebrows, firm, regular mouth. How like Hilary Frome to pick an incipient stunner. In a second she had looked down again, and then she said:

'Well, perhaps the other too.'

'You were cooling off?'

'He was. We weren't going out much anymore. Before, we were going out all the time. Discos and dances and concerts and things. You know. But recently . . .'

She suddenly spotted the little pile of personal things that Pumfrey had retrieved from Hilary Frome's room, and she snatched at the tiny Boots' pocket diary.

'See—look!' She fumbled with it, and opened it at January. As Pumfrey had thought at a cursory glance, the diary did not appear to be any different from most such pocket diaries: monumentally unrevealing. But when the girl pointed he saw in all the weeks of January the initials MW, and sometimes a time, marked against day after day. At least twice a week, sometimes more.

'You see. We were going together all the time. The other girls were awfully jealous, really sick. He was so dishy. And so . . . remote. They'd have given their eye teeth to get him away from me . . . I wonder who did.'

'You think someone got him away?'

'I suppose so. You see, in February we didn't get out together so much. And then in March . . . He kept making excuses . . . He said he had something on, always something on. Some cow or other stole him.'

Pumfrey looked at the later entries. He saw the initials MP against the preceding Sunday.

'Somebody, at any rate,' he said. 'So, you didn't formally break it off, then? He never told you what he had on?'

'No. He just went . . . sort of remote. With some girls he made dates, pretending to be all enthusiastic, and then just didn't turn up. We used to have a good giggle, thinking of them waiting.'

'I can imagine,' said Pumfrey, thinking of Onyx Muggeridge.

'I was sort of glad he didn't do that to me. But I knew he must have got interested in somebody else.'

'Perhaps you're right,' said Pumfrey sympathetically, trying to think back to the pains of his own adolescence. 'Can you tell me something about Hilary Frome? I've heard a lot about him, but not much from his own age group.'

'Oh—he was wonderful. So cool. Like ice. Marvellous. He could just stand there, you know, and I'd look at him, and shivers would go down my spine.'

Pumfrey could easily imagine it.

'He had such control. Over himself, over everyone around him. I mean, he never needed anybody, you know? He took what he wanted. And he was so confident. It was so marvellous just being with him, having the others see me with him . . .'

'What did you talk about?'

'Talk? Oh—you know: music and that. He always knew the sounds that were just coming in, always on the ball, long before the others. And of course we talked about school. He hated this place. I mean, he despised it. It was just beneath him, coming here. He was too big for Burleigh, and he knew it.'

'Did he talk much about the teachers?'

'Oh yes. He talked about all of them at one time or other. The head he just strung along, did a great big act for. He didn't care a damn for the rest.'

'Who did he talk about particularly?'

'Like who did he hate, you mean? Well, Makepeace he just despised. He thought he was the feeblest thing he'd ever seen. He used to drive him to desperation, you know, he just put the knife in—'

'Why?'

She opened her eyes. Apparently it was a silly question.

'Well, like I said, he despised him. I mean, if a teacher can't keep order, he's no good, is he? Hilary never liked weak people. It was the same with that Corbett Farraday. Hilary's father was having to give him tuition to make up for Farraday's lousy teaching. Hilary used to say:"Marvellous. Dad pays a thou a year for me to go there, and then he has to do the teaching himself."The only one he had a good word for was Miss Grower.'

'Oh? Why Miss Grower? Did he respect her?'

'As a teacher. Oh yes, he did. He wasn't really interested in history, but he said her classes were fabulous. And she did World Religions, too, and she didn't do all that Christian stuff—most of these teachers just get you reading rotten old parables and things from the New Testament, and telling them what you think they meant, as if anyone cared. But he said she would go into Hinduism, and Buddhism, and all sorts of queer things like Thuggee and Zoro—Zoro-something-or-other. He thought she was trying to take the mickey out of religion altogether, because she was forced to take the subject and she thought it beneath her. He liked that. He thought it was a fabulous thing to do. He asked me to get anything I could on her, but I never managed to.'

'He asked you *what?*'

'To get anything on her.' She opened her eyes at him, as if it was the most normal thing in the world, and he was being particularly dim. 'Like she's a lesbian, you know. And he wanted to know if she'd made up to any of the girls around here.'

'Why would he want to know that?'

'Well, to get a hold on her, of course. He used to say "All power enriches, and absolute power enriches absol-

utely." It was some old saying, or something. He liked
knowing things about people, even about other boys at
school. And if he'd got anything on the Grower, he could
have used it with his father.'

'I'm sorry. I know you think I'm slow. But how would
he have used evidence about Miss Grower's . . . supposed
tastes with his father?'

'Oh, you know Dr Frome. Don't you? I mean, he was
terribly ambitious for Hilary. I mean, *terribly*. It had
started in the last year or two, when Hilary had grown up,
and was so . . . striking, you know. He saw that Hilary
could be something. He'd like to have taken Hilary away
and sent him to a Public School, but it was too late by
then. Hilary saw that if he was going to get anywhere,
he'd have to go to Cullbridge Comprehensive. But his
father was very stiff-necked, you know, because he'd
refused to send him there four years ago, and he didn't
like admitting he'd been wrong. So Hilary collected data
on Burleigh, to try and make him change his mind. But
when old Crumwallis offered to make Hilary head boy,
his dad dug his heels in. I mean, he was creepy at times,
his dad.'

'Creepy? I didn't notice anything creepy about him.'

'Didn't you? I can tell you, I did. When Hilary took me
home, they just looked me over — well, not his mum, so
much, but his dad — to see if I was good enough. Like an
inspection, you know. And they asked about my parents,
and that, and my dad works for an estate agent's in
Cullbridge, and I don't think that was good enough. I
mean, he was so ambitious . . . And then, if anyone made
any complaints about Hilary —'

'Oh. Did people make complaints about Hilary?'

'Oh, one or two did. Like the father of one of the
younger boys at Burleigh went along to Dr Frome last
year to complain that Hilary had been bullying his little
lad. Isn't that feeble? I mean, doing something like that?

Hilary'd just been playing with the kid, really, just teasing him, you know? The father knew he wouldn't get anywhere if he went to old Crumwallis, so he went to Hilary's dad instead.'

'What happened?'

'Oh, Hilary's dad really bawled him out. I mean, really made it hot for him, you know? He got on his high horse, told him to take it to the headmaster if he thought he had any complaint, told him if there was nothing in it he'd sue him for slander, warned him not to say anything to anyone else or he'd have him in the courts, showed him the door, and all that. That's what I mean, it was creepy. He hated anything that got in Hilary's way. He'd have done anything to make sure Hilary got ahead.'

'And that bothered Hilary, did it?'

'Well, it did a bit. I mean, Hilary wanted to get ahead, naturally, and he would've. But he could see his dad was all uptight about it, and going about it in the wrong way.'

'I see. Tell me, what did Hilary think about this idea that he would be head boy next year?'

'He thought it was a laugh. And a dead bind, too. I mean, when he first heard about it, he was really cheesed off. It was like the headmaster had put one over on him, wasn't it? And he rather wished he'd treated the head like he'd treated all the rest of the creeps here. Those were his words, Hilary's. But then he thought about it a bit, and he saw there might be possibilities. I mean, he still wanted to leave and have his GCE year at the Comprehensive, but he didn't want to burn his boats, you know. He thought that being head boy might be a real giggle . . .'

'What sort of thing was he planning to do?'

'Well, I mean, really wreck the school, but in a sort of clever way, so that old Crumwallis thought he was doing a splendid job, and was egging him on to do all sorts of things that he knew would bring the school down around the head's ears. He hadn't really worked it out, but it could have been a gas. He was so clever, so inventive, was Hilary.'

'He certainly seems to have had a fertile mind.'

'Oh, he did. I hope . . .'

'Yes?'

'I hope his child has it too . . . Because I think I'm going to have Hilary's child.'

CHAPTER 15

SUGGESTIONS AND DISCOVERIES

When he had bundled Margaret Wilkinson off home, in the care of Penny Warlock, Mike Pumfrey burrowed deeper into his comfortable desk chair and raised his eyebrows at Sergeant Fenniway.

'Poor kid,' he said. 'I mean, you know, poor kid.'

Sergeant Fenniway seemed to think he was being heartless.

'She's going through a rough time.'

'Of course she's going through a rough time. I don't see why that should make her talk like a human word-processor.'

'Don't your kids talk like that?'

'Pretty much,' admitted Pumfrey. 'I suppose the schools have given up caring. Occasionally mine say something quite funny as well. My daughter the other day said one of her friends "wasn't as pregnant as she thinks she is." I hope the same is true of that poor little thing. The illegitimate child of Hilary Frome starts off with two pretty nasty black marks against it before it even arrives in the world.'

'It didn't sound very certain to me,' said Fenniway.

'Nor to me either . . . It'd be interesting to see whether

the Fromes acknowledged it. I'd be willing to bet they wouldn't. Not if what she told us is half-way true.'

Pumfrey picked up off the desk, where Margaret Wilkinson had left it, Hilary Frome's diary. He really should have looked more closely at it before. He began leafing through the pages for the first three months of the year. As he read the cursory entries, he pursed his lips, and the brown toothbrush above his lips began to quiver with life.

'At least this thing begins to make a bit more sense now. Most of it's just dates and engagements, as far as I can see. Look at this, Fenniway: I think he's got a little code for girls he intends to stand up. He puts a tiny skull and crossbones after their initials. Sarky little swine. I bet . . . yes, look: the night he died, Thursday, 29th March, has 'OM, Sports Pavilion', then the skull and crossbones in a different pen. I suppose that must mean that he originally intended to meet her, then changed his mind when Crumwallis asked him to take over the boarding section that evening.'

'Anything else of interest?' asked Fenniway.

'Hmmm. Pickerage on Sunday—and occasional dates elsewhere, some during school time. Trips to the lavatories, do you suppose? How little boys' schools change, after all. There are one or two other names that come more than once: PQ and TW. Quigly was the name of one of his pals—one of his conspicuously few pals—that his mother mentioned. Quigly and Willis. I suppose those are the two. Nothing much else that I can . . . That's a bit odd, though. Occasional single letters. V on March 22nd, R on the 26th. Don't suppose it means anything, but all the other names are given two initials, so you'd think these would be even closer friends. Yet they're only mentioned once.'

'Anything about any of the teachers?'

'That's a point. Wait a bit: here's a GG. That could

only be Miss Grower, surely. Here are several PMs . . .
Ah, and here's a DG. Those all must be teachers, don't
you think? When did Miss Gilberd say he made that
clever little scene in the delicatessen? Monday, that's it.
And on Monday the 26th here's her initials, along with
that initial R—which has no time by it, and neither do
the teacher's names. In other words, when he has enjoyed
one of his little triumphs over one of the teachers, he
notes it down in his diary.'

'As you say, a right little charmer.'

Pumfrey banged the little book shut with a sharp blow
of his fist.

'Ugh! In this job you have to stamp hard on any feeling
that whoever did it has rid the world of a reptile, and
done it a real service. Even if, as seems likely, in this
case they did it inadvertently. What now, Fenniway?
What further ornament to the race is there to interview?'

'Well, there is the Muggeridge woman.'

'Oh God, there is, too. I wonder if we need to see her.
After all, he clearly didn't keep the date.'

'Still, he made it. It sounds as if they were talking for
quite a time, from what Muggeridge said. Of course, they
probably did it just to cheese him off, humiliate him
in front of the littlies. But something might have been
said . . .'

Pumfrey sighed.

'I suppose so. I rather hoped that one lousy mother a
day might be considered a reasonable ration. You do
keep me up to the mark, Fenniway. Still—it surely
needn't take more than a few minutes. What's the time,
by the way? Nearly four. Let's go right away: we might
get in and out before that sweaty oaf gets back home
himself.'

They collected their things, locked up the study, and
went through the door that led into the older part of the
school. The boys had mostly gone in the last quarter of an

hour, enthusiastic to spread the news in the coffee bars
and through the groups of street-corner loungers (groups
which Mr Crumwallis had been very down on, in the days
of his prosperity). The older boys expected to accumulate
considerable cachet by recounting the story of Hilary
Frome's last minutes to the girls of St Mary's or (at a
pinch) the Comprehensive girls, who mostly were tied up
with boys at their own school, but could on rare occasions
be tempted away. The corridors of Burleigh were deserted.
It was as they were passing up the passage that led
towards the front door that Pumfrey heard voices, and
motioned to Fenniway to stop and keep quiet. What he
had heard was the continuation of a discussion that had
been going on in the Staff Common Room since school
finished.

'I don't care what you say, I think it's pretty odd, those
two taking over the school like that at the drop of a hat.
Taking advantage, I call it, and I've no liking for Crumwallis. It's almost as if they planned it.'

The voice was Bill Muggeridge, instinct as usual with a
dull and unspecified grudge. The next was Tom Tedder's.

'Come off it, Bill: don't try to be subtle, it doesn't
become you. Why not say right out that they've been
planning these things to ease the Crumwallises out, and
get the school at a price they can afford?'

'I didn't say that.'

'Well, I do feel,' came the high, self-assured voice of
Glenda Grower, 'that you're looking a gift horse in the
mouth. All of us would rather work for Sep than that
addle-pated fraud Crumwallis, and I for one don't see
Sep or McWhirter wading through slaughter to a throne.
Is Burleigh really worth a corpse?'

'Perhaps they didn't mean the corpse,' resumed the
obstinate voice of Bill. 'Perhaps they just didn't know
about poisons. We're not all like Corbett.'

'Oh, I say, half a mo . . .'

'Do you think it weally will be better under Coffin?' came an unmistakable lisp. 'I mean, he's tewibly *sarcastic*, and iwonic, and that, and he has awfully high standards. Will we weally be *safe*? I should think he could be absolutely *woothless!*'

'What precisely,' asked Glenda, 'do you mean to imply by that, Percy?'

'Nothing!' came the agitated voice. 'Nothing at all. I'm just talking about possible sackings—though I suppose he will call them wedundancies . . .'

'Well, I agree with Glenda,' said the more pacific voice of Dorothea Gilberd. 'I think some of you are being horribly ungrateful. After all, if the Crumwallises had been in charge for another fortnight, we would all have been out of a job next term. Sep may have played his cards closely, but he's really saved our bacon.'

'I wouldn't be too sure of *that*, old girl,' came the relentlessly jolly voice of Corbett Farraday. Pumfrey could guess how much Dorothea Gilberd liked being called 'old girl'. 'From what I hear, Dr Frome has been cooking our goose, whatever good old Sep may have been doing with our bacon.'

'What do you mean? How do you know?'

'One of my parents—mother of Gillies in 3B—came to see me as soon as school finished. All this worried mother hen stuff. She says that Frome has been going on about the school to anyone who has rung up to offer condolences. Not many have, of course: too bally awkward. But some of them have been parents, and of course they've passed it on, and it's spreading like wildfire.'

'Hence all the phone calls to the school, I suppose. What's he been saying?'

'Pretty much what you might expect. Telling them how much he blames himself, how he knew Mrs C. was incompetent and a menace, how it will need more than a new head to knock the school into shape, telling them not to make his mistake, get their little Jonnnies out before it's too late . . .'

'My God,' said Tom Tedder. 'He seems to be doing a thorough job.'

'He seems to me,' said Glenda Grower authoritatively, 'to be very definitely jumping the gun. I never thought to put in a good word for Mother C., but as far as I've heard, no one has proved it was her negligence or slovenliness killed the boy.'

'From what I've heard,' said Tom Tedder, 'it was certainly deliberate. Poison put into the bottle.'

'Either way,' said Corbett Farraday, 'that leaves Mrs C. with her trousers down. Sorry, skirts. Nobody but a lunatic would have left that bottle out in the corridor all day.'

'No,' admitted Glenda. 'Oh, I can see the man has a pretty big grievance against the Crumwallises. But he does seem to be over-reacting as far as the school as a whole is concerned. Sort of protecting himself, in a way. Because after all, he was pretty chuffed to have the apple of his eye designated as the next head boy, wasn't he? And that was only a couple of weeks ago.'

'I expect that's *why* he's over-reacting, wouldn't you think?' came the sensible voice of Miss Gilberd. 'Because in a way he had been giving the school his seal of approval. I only hope the other parents manage to see it for what it is.'

'I suppose they may when they sit down and think it over,' said Glenda Grower. 'After all, several of the parents have probably got a better idea of what kind of a thug Hilary Frome was than his doting parents seem to have had. There were those that complained to his father about him last year, remember. Boys talk, you know, and some of the mums and dads may well have realized that Hilary was behind all the riot and brouhaha that went on around this place.'

'Quite apart,' said Makepeace, 'from what one suspects went on now and then in the lavatwies.'

'That's a point,' said Tom Tedder. 'That's really a point. After all, some of the parents could have made a nasty stink if they'd known a bit on that subject. That would really have cooked Hilary's goose. Not, I suppose, that any of the boys would willingly have told, but it might have come out if the boys had been upset by it. Who did he go with? Wattling, I suspect. And of course poor old Pickerage . . .'

'I say,' came the voice of Corbett Farraday, 'you don't suppose Mother Pickerage was trying to blackmail Dr Frome, do you? And he got hold of a cachet of instant poison—who better? it seems to have worked much faster than anything I know of—and slipped it into Pickerage's medicine to keep the thing quiet.'

'More to the point, I should have thought, to have slipped it to Pickerage's Mum,' said Glenda Grower. 'Which would have desolated nobody, least of all poor little Malcolm. Come on, let's go home. This is getting us fast into Cloud Cuckoo Land.'

'No, but you know, poor little Malcolm has been looking pretty peaky these last few days,' pursued Corbett Farraday, like a puppy at a bone much too big for it. 'Not just since the murder. He's been sort of thoughtful for days. I noticed it on Monday. I'm sure something must have happened to him over the weekend.'

Bill Muggeridge let out a coarse suggestion, which, like so many coarse suggestions, was in fact nothing but the truth.

'*Really*, Bill,' came Dorothea Gilberd's shocked tones. 'You really do . . . Sometimes I . . . Anyway, I won't believe it . . . I'm sure it was something else altogether . . . I'm sure if someone sympathetic could only *talk* to Malcolm . . .'

There were signs from the Common Room of chairs being

pushed back, of bags and books being collected. Pumfrey gave a sign to Fenniway and they both darted up the corridor and evaporated through the front door. Once outside on the driveway, Pumfrey took a deep breath of fresh air, and then, contrarily, took out his pipe and began stuffing it with tobacco.

'Well!' he said. 'That was interesting.'

'Was it?' said Fenniway, creasing his forehead. 'Just a lot of speculation really, wasn't it? Some of it was possibilities we've been over already ourselves, and most of the rest was just fantastic.'

'The speculations of suspects are usually pretty revealing,' said Pumfrey, puffing thoughtfully. 'What they do and what they don't speculate on. And then there was that about the poison: something we'd thought about earlier, and which we should have remembered when we heard the aconite was in the medicine, not the sherry. I'm kicking myself that it slipped my mind.'

Pumfrey walked moodily along the gravel, stubbing his toes into the sandy path. The puffs of smoke rose hectically from his pipe. He walked up and down for several minutes, doing no more than nod at the teachers as they departed one by one. Finally he turned back to Fenniway.

'I'm not sure that we'll bother with that Muggeridge woman just yet,' he said.

'Oh? Well, if you say so. Do you mind telling me what it is that you've remembered?'

'No. No, I don't, now I've thought it through. Look here, it seems to me that there are two odd things about what happened here last night. Two questions that we ought to have asked ourselves. Here's question number one: why did Hilary Frome insist on—'

'Excuse me.'

Mike Pumfrey stopped in his tracks. Looking up at him was a brown, Indian face, surmounting the green blazer and short flannel trousers that were the Burleigh required wear.

'Hello. Who are you, then?'

'I'm Patel. I'm in 3A.'

Patel was not one of those foreign boys for whom their parents were misguided enough to pay (specially inflated) fees on the assumption that they were giving their heirs an English Public School education. Patel's father owned a supermarket on the outskirts of Cullbridge, and an Indian delicatessen that supplied most of the best Indian restaurants in a fifty mile radius, as well as catering for the few Cullbridge housewives who gingerly experimented at giving their cooking a modestly oriental flavour. Patel's father was a first-rate businessman, but his understanding of English institutions was still under-ripe, hence his pride in the private education he was giving his son. But young Patel was very bright, and he was getting the message through: it was unlikely that for his younger sons Mr Patel would lay out so much for so little.

'Well, Patel of 3A, what can we do for you?'

'I don't suppose it's anything of real importance,' said Patel in his perfect English that unfairly sounded more charming for coming from an apparently foreign mouth. 'But you see, I read detective stories, and there they say that every little thing has importance in an investigation. I wondered whether that was true in real life?'

'Well,' said Pumfrey, considering. 'Perhaps not every little thing, no. You have to discard a lot. On the other hand, we obviously have to know every little thing, so that we can decide whether it's important or not.'

'Yes,' said Patel seriously. 'Yes, I see.'

'So if you've got anything that you think just *might* have something to do with this—'

'Yes. Well, it can't do any harm, I suppose. You see, it's like this. The boys are saying that all these things that have been happening around here are probably connected. Is that right?'

'We don't quite know yet. They might be.'

'You see, after the last Parents' Evening—you've heard what happened then, have you?'

'Yes. The boarders got rather drunk.'

'That's right. They looked *awful* the next morning. Well, the next day I was kept in, and so I was walking home on my own. And as I was going down the drive here, I saw a bottle—a bottle of vodka.'

'Ah! Where was that?'

'In the undergrowth round the trees over there. I'll show you.'

They began walking down the drive. Mr Makepeace, the last teacher to depart, watched them curiously, and then looked airily the other way. Patel stopped half-way up the drive.

'It was about there, see? And I thought that if it was found, it might get someone into trouble. Because it wasn't hidden, or anything. So I just kicked it further into the undergrowth.'

'Did you, now? Do you remember which direction you kicked it in?'

'Oh—I suppose towards that thick stuff over there. To keep it hidden, you know.'

Together the three of them went gingerly in the direction of the stout old tree and the massed jungle of weeds around its base. They circled round it carefully, Pumfrey warning Patel from any over-enthusiastic plunges into the undergrowth. Finally it was Fenniway who pointed, and there, nestling under nettles, they saw the bottle with the Russian imperial crown on it. It was empty. Pumfrey took out a plastic bag from his pocket. He secured the bottle round the neck with a piece of string. Then he pulled it from the surrounding greenery and put it into his bag.

'Thank you, Patel,' he said. 'I think this might be important. And I think I know whose fingerprints are going to be found on it. Thank God we've had fine weather all this week. That's the first bit of luck we've had in this case.'

CHAPTER 16

TRUTH

It was after nine when the results came through from the labs. Fenniway had been up to the dormitories to see if Pickerage was back from his dinner with his mother, and when he returned empty-handed, Pumfrey was picking up the phone.

'Yes? You've got them? Good . . . Smudged, are they? No, I'm not surprised . . . Ah—they're Dr Frome's, are they? . . . Yes, I did . . . How did you come to have his prints, by the way? . . . Just one of these hysterical women patient cases, you mean? . . . Oh yes. Sure. They happen all the time . . . It wasn't taken seriously? . . . Well, you've been very good. I appreciate it. I wanted to get it settled tonight . . . Yes, I think it pretty much sews it up . . . 'Bye.'

He slapped down the phone.

'Hear that?'

'Yes,' said Fenniway. He was a cautious, steady soul, and so he added: 'But it doesn't sew it up quite as neatly as you made out, does it?'

'No. I know,' said Pumfrey. 'Malcolm back yet?'

'No. He phoned Toby to say that his mother was taking him out to the pictures.'

'Good God. What's got into her?'

'It's probably *The Stud*, or something. Perhaps she's trying to pump all the info she can out of him, for use on her cocktail circuit.'

'I wouldn't be surprised. But she's a nuisance. It's us who ought to be doing the pumping, and we'd be a good deal better at it, I should think. That's what I'd like to be doing now. Still . . .'

Fenniway waited. When Pumfrey was near the end of a case he tended towards the impetuous. Fenniway was willing to bet what the next step would be.

'Still, I don't think it need stop us. Let's get along there now.'

Fenniway knew better than to urge caution. He could just picture the bristling of the moustache, the glare of the eyes if he did. He accepted the inevitable.

'Shall we clear up here?' he asked.

'Just take the vital things. We'll have to come back tomorrow—to see Pickerage, inform Coffin. He'll be pleased, by the way.'

'Unless he was counting on it being one of the hopeless teachers.'

'That would have been bad for the school in the short term, however terrible a teacher he was. And Coffin's having to think in the short term at the moment. No, this will be better. Coffin will be delighted.'

Pumfrey packed up the desk, put into his briefcase his folder, his notes, Hilary Frome's diary and the assembled bric-à-brac of the case. Then they put on their coats and went to the door. Before he put the lights out, Pumfrey looked round.

'Well,' he said, still scowling at the room in dissatisfaction, 'I hope the first thing Coffin does is put these books into some kind of order.'

'Anybody'd think you were Hercule Poirot,' said Fenniway.

Then the light went out, symbolically extinguishing Edward Crumwallis and all his works. Pumfrey locked the study door, and the two of them went out to the police car.

As they drove towards Maple Grove Fenniway tried, in his steady way, to put a damper on his superior's inbred precipitancy. Moral certainty on their part, Fenniway felt, really got them very little of the way.

'It's not going to be easy,' he said tentatively.

Pumfrey swivelled round at him.

'Trying to rein me in?' he grunted. 'I know you, Fenniway. You think I have a headlong tendency, don't you? God, it sounds like a splinter group in the Labour Party. Well, I tell you, I want to get this over and I intend to. Loose ends we can tie up in the morning.' Then he conceded Fenniway's point. 'No, it's not going to be easy. Damned sticky, in fact, if he takes the line I expect.'

'I suppose you'll have to play it slow? Lead up to it carefully? He's obviously no shirker when it comes to threatening court actions and the like. He could be on to the Chief Constable in two shakes of a bunny's tail.'

'He could indeed,' admitted Pumfrey. 'That was interesting, what Margaret Wilkinson was telling us. A chap who's that quick with the slander action has got something to hide. I think I heard something about some faulty diagnosis some time ago . . .'

'Yes, I did too,' said Fenniway. 'Not really relevant, though.'

'No, of course not. But he's obviously jumpy. As to how I'm going to play it, I suppose it will be by ear. It usually is. It's not as though we're without evidence.'

'There's the bottle,' conceded Fenniway, who in fact thought their case paper-thin. 'Though that's far from conclusive, isn't it? There's the diary—ditto. We hope there'll be something from Pickerage, but we haven't got it yet.'

'There's the question of access to poison.'

'His having had access doesn't prove anything, does it, sir? It doesn't add up to a great deal, taken as a whole.'

'There are my two questions. Nothing concrete in them,

but to my mind they speak volumes. And they ought to lead us to some real evidence. But we'll have to see. As far as I'm concerned, I want to put the case to bed tonight. But at the worst I'll just bring it out into the open. We'll certainly have work to do in the next few days . . .' He peered out into the darkness, at the large, detached residences they were passing. 'I think this is what they call a nice area, isn't it? To me it's the most boring part of Cullbridge. Funny, you know, but I think the Fromes are pretty boring people too. Odd, isn't it?'

They drew up outside *Deauville*. Through the hedge, clipped into the shape of guardsmen's busbies, they saw lights in the living-room. There was not a sound coming from the house.

'Right,' said Pumfrey, looking at Fenniway. 'Let's get it done.'

They shut the car door softly, opened the gate, and walked up the path. They listened for a moment at the door, and then rang the bell. The silence was suffocating. All the street seemed to have gone into mute mourning, in sympathy. The two men almost welcomed the sound of footsteps in the hall.

'Oh—Superintendent.'

Mrs Frome had done something to her hair, and put a light make-up on. But she seemed still as if she were drained. Some essential life appeared to have been sucked out of her, and she seemed almost fearful. Was she anticipating further horrors to come?

'Will you come in? I hope you'll excuse . . .'

Her voice trailed away as she led them into the hall.

'I'm grateful that you . . .'

But again it faded as she ushered them towards the living-room.

She opened the door. In a far corner, under a standard lamp, Dr Frome was sitting. His face was flushed and gleaming, and there was a glass of whisky on the table at

his side. Over the room there hung a smell of grief, and
stale smoke, and drink. Frome's eyes were red and tired
as he peered at his wife, and then made out the figures
in the shadow behind her.

'It's the Superintendent, dear—'

Frome pushed himself forward and got up. He was not
altogether steady, but his eyes began to gleam, and he
could hardly control the excitement in his voice, which
quivered, even though he was speaking quite unnaturally
loudly.

'Superintendent. Good of you to come round. Has anything come up? Have you got results? Can you give me the
name of the bastard who killed my son?'

'Yes, Dr Frome, I can,' said Mike Pumfrey. 'I'm afraid
that your son unwittingly killed himself.'

CHAPTER 17

LIFE AFTER DEATH

It is not easy to celebrate the solution of a murder case
without seeming at the same time to celebrate the death
of the victim. In the case of the murder of Hilary Frome
that consideration seemed to the staff members of Burleigh School to have less than the usual weight. At any
rate, on Saturday morning they went right ahead and
celebrated.

They did it tactfully. When Septimus Coffin rang
round to some of them to tell them the outcome of the
police investigations, the favoured few then began ringing
round to the others, and the outcome of all the intense
exchanging of confidences was a decision to meet at
lunch-time in a little-frequented saloon bar in a dark
side-street down from the bus station. It was a drinking

place highly unlikely to be frequented by any parents who might look askance at a degree of modest revelry over the death of Hilary Frome.

In fact, celebration was not the first priority, though Percy Makepeace was, it is true, inclined to attribute the entire affair to divine intervention. What they really wanted — like any Sunday newspaper reader — was information, details, the background fill-in. A lunch-time Cornish pasty, a pint of bitter or a gin and something, rendered piquant by acres of speculation and circumstantial detail — these seemed the most desirable thing in the world, to relieve the tensions of the last few days. They were glad when Septimus Coffin promised to absent himself for a few minutes from his Herculean task of rebuilding the temple, for it was Septimus who had enjoyed the confidences of Superintendent Pumfrey. So at half past twelve they were all there, even Iain McWhirter, who had never before been known to grace the inside of a public house, but who shuffled in five minutes before the appointed time, ordered a gin and angostura, and huddled on a bench by the fire, snuffling delightedly to himself.

'Poetic justice!' he chortled. 'Never did I think to see it so beautifully exemplified, so close at hand.'

Others were more seemly in their satisfaction, particularly Septimus Coffin. The mantle of headmasterhood sat lightly on him, but sit it did. He collected a Scotch and water, and sat down at the little table by the fire, insisting that he could only stay a few minutes.

'Duty calls,' he said, 'the business of saving your jobs and mine on the foundering vessel forsaken by the Crumwallises. There are parents to ring, ruffled feathers to smooth, domestic details to be ironed out —'

'Then shoot,' said Glenda Grower, as direct as she was impatient. 'How do they know he did it himself?'

'Ah well, that seems to be the only possible deduction

from the evidence,' said Septimus, expansive and expository, as if outlining the strategic decisions taken by Caesar at the climax of a battle against the Gauls. 'I feel the Superintendent was remarkably clever here. He tells me that right from the start he posed to himself two questions.' (Here it may be noted that Mike Pumfrey was less than totally honest with Septimus Coffin. It was only right at the end of the investigation that the two questions had formulated themselves for him with any clarity. Policemen, however, even in these degenerate times, must be allowed their professional pride, especially when dealing with schoolteachers.) 'These questions were: "Why did Hilary Frome insist on Pickerage taking his medicine?" and "How come the poison worked so fast?" Now they solved the second, initially, by assuming that it was in the sherry, because they knew Hilary had had one while he was downstairs. But the discovery that the poison was in the medicine blew that one to smithereens.'

'But don't some poisons sometimes work more or less instantly?' queried Dorothea Gilberd. 'They do in books.'

'Because it's a jolly sight more exciting that way,' said Corbett Farraday. 'Not many of them do in fact, unless you've got a wonky heart, which I'm sure Hilary Frome hadn't.'

'Oh, Hilary had a very wonky heart,' said Septimus, 'but only in the more sentimental meaning of the term. No, Corbett is right: hardly any poison works like that, and certainly not any of the aconite-related ones. Now one answer could have been that the poison was—through Mrs C.'s inefficiency—in the glass that Hilary took down when he went to get the sherry. But Mrs C.'s medicaments were almost all of a virtually harmless nature, and the fact is that the poison was in the medicine bottle as well. The only other answer, then, was that Hilary started vomiting and heaving because he knew what he had drunk, and was trying to get rid of it.'

'What an *awful* moment for him,' said Dorothea.

'My heart bleeds,' said Glenda. 'Go on, Sep.'

'Now, to go back to the first question: that too leads one back to Hilary. We all know what Hilary's attitude to Burleigh School was, and by the time Pumfrey had finished he had a good idea as well. Hilary always made a great big V sign at the place, and all its rules and personnel. And Pickerage was his friend. Yet suddenly here he was insisting that Pickerage take some perfectly useless medicine prescribed by Mrs Crumwallis, when normally he would have been quite happy to have poured it down the sink—would have insisted on doing so, in fact, as a gesture of defiance. Why? And the only answer possible was because that it was he who poisoned it.'

'But it *is* so horrible,' insisted Dorothea Gilberd. 'I mean, they were *friends*. Why would he do a thing like that to *Malcolm?*'

'One thing I'd bet,' said Penny. 'It was part of a campaign to ruin the school, wasn't it? So that his parents would take him away and put him in the Comprehensive.'

'That's it. A campaign that was going to increase in seriousness the longer it had to go. So the first stage was something quite innocuous, something that looked like nothing more than a schoolboy jape from the old *Magnet*: he took a bottle of vodka from his father's apparently copious store and laced the boarders' fruit cup with it. It was never missed, but his father's prints were on it, some of them smudged with his own gloved ones. Thanks to Toby, that little episode was completely hushed up.'

'Due entirely to the quick thinking of Mr Crumwallis,' said Toby. 'As he told us himself, frequently.'

'Quite. *Requiescat in pace*, you monumental old fraud. So Hilary put a little V for vodka in his diary, and goes back to the drawing-board. But then he made a mistake.'

'I know!' said Glenda. 'I bet I know. He tried to recruit

Malcolm. People always thought Malcolm was his lieutenant, but they never could point to anything he'd actually done.'

'That's it. Last Sunday they took the day off together and went to Stanhope Woods. And among other things, which I won't go into, Hilary told Pickerage about his campaign, in a suitably edited version, I would guess, and told him he wanted him to hide a razor-blade in Wattling's flannel, and put a bit of glass into some suitable dish prepared by Mrs Garfitt: shepherd's pie, fish cakes or whatever.'

'And Malcolm refused?'

'Yes. Poor little chap—it's sad really: he said, "It's the only home I've got," and dug his heels in. After all, he's a bright enough little chap, even if he is ignorant as hell, and he knew that if someone tries to swallow glass they can quite easily kill themselves, and almost certainly would give themselves a nasty injury. He knew that if it was just stuck into the pie it could be anyone who copped it. It could be one of his pals, just as he knew that Wattling could really get his face carved up through Hilary's plans. And nothing Hilary could say would persuade him.'

'I always said that Malcolm was straight,' said Toby.

'I think we all felt that. But the police had this idea the whole time that Pickerage was holding out on them, keeping something back. They'd get something new out of him, and then there would still seem something more. Because the fact is, though he was upset at being asked to do that by Hilary Frome, Hilary was still his big god, right up to the time he died. He held back about what he'd been asked to do partly out of instinct, because a schoolkid knows things like that get him into trouble, but partly too out of loyalty to Hilary.'

'Talk about loyalty being bloody misplaced,' said Bill Muggeridge, taking a great swig of his bitter.

'But I bet there was something else,' said Glenda Grower. 'I bet there was some idea at the back of his mind that Hilary must have tried to poison him.'

'I think there probably was. But that was something I don't think he was even admitting to himself. But he did give himself away in one respect. Yesterday he had his lunch upstairs in the boarding annexe. The constable on duty there said he mashed over every mouthful he ate. Now this was before poor old Harris started spewing blood all over the dining hall. If Malcolm was still suspicious of an attempt on him, he would surely have suspected *poison*. And in that case mashing up the stuff wouldn't have done one iota of good.

'He knew Hilary had done the razor-blade trick himself. He knew the boarding annexe routine, and he'd slipped in in school time. R for razor-blade in the diary. The next day, Tuesday, he shoved the glass in the shepherd's pie that Mrs Garfitt had made. But she froze it down, and he was disappointed of his sensation. I rather think that by now Hilary must have been rather hepped up on the whole idea of death. I think he had some kind of cold fever on him, and the only thing that could cool it was a death. And of course a death was one way he could be absolutely sure that the school would be at the centre of a storm of dreadful, damaging publicity.'

'And Fate delivered Pickerage into his hands,' said Corbett Farraday portentously.

'It did. Clever old Fate,' said Septimus. 'With his medicine standing outside in the corridor, so that just anyone could have tampered with it. But I suspect that, whether or not Malcolm had been consigned by Fate to the sick room, he was in any case the chosen victim.'

'But why? That's horrible!' protested Dorothea Gilberd. 'He was his friend.'

'People don't do things like that!' protested Percy Makepeace.

'Most people don't do murder at all,' said Septimus. 'And Malcolm marked himself out because he knew of Hilary's plans. Even if he had not confided in Malcolm about a possible murder, Malcolm knew he was responsible for the other things. A great man can trust his disciples only so far. And a fifteen-year-old boy knows perfectly well that a thirteen-year-old can have knowledge winkled out of him. So if murder was to be done, Malcolm was the obvious victim. Quite apart from the possibility that Hilary relished the wiping out of a disciple whose devotion had proved to be less than total. You talk about his being Hilary's friend. But did Hilary have any friends? I don't think any relationship where emotion was involved ever entered his mind. No, I really don't think there was the least hesitation in Frome's mind when, as Corbett poetically observed, Fate delivered Malcolm into his hands.'

'I don't like this,' shivered Penny.

'One thing about how the whole thing is going to be presented to the public by the police, at the inquest and by us. It will be quite easy to argue that Hilary had no idea of the strength of the aconite he had put into the medicine. He'd abstracted it from his father's office at the hospital, during one of the teaching sessions he had with him there—Dr Frome was . . . er . . . supplementing the science teaching.'

'I sayl Bally cheek,' said Corbett Farraday.

'Hilary—the idea is ironic—was thinking of becoming a doctor. Naturally he needed special coaching. He went around to his father at the hospital after school, and understandably enough his father was often called away. But it will be quite possible to argue that he had no idea of the strength and effect of the stuff he used. That this was just one more in a series of japes. I am fairly sure that the police will spare the feelings of Dr and Mrs Frome, and suggest at the inquest that this was what happened.

"Death by misadventure" the jury can bring in.'

There came a delirious snuffling sound, rising to a squeak, from Mr McWhirter, who sounded like a piglet who had just discovered a chocolate box.

'There is, I fear, one thing against such a theory.'

'Quite,' said Septimus.

'But what?' said Dorothea. 'I mean, really, I can believe that much more easily than I can believe in a boy of that age actually deciding to murder his best friend.'

'You are forgetting,' wheezed Mr McWhirter, 'the vodka bottle. Why would he use gloves if he didn't already have murder in mind? He could hardly have imagined that the headmaster would call in all the resources of forensic science if it was just a case of a mere school jape.'

'Quite,' repeated Septimus. 'But I think it will be for the good of the school if we accept the alternative explanation, at least for public consumption. Make it a party line, in fact. It makes things easier for Dr and Mrs Frome, to say nothing of ourselves.' He pushed his chair back, regretfully, but not too regretfully. 'As for me, I must get back to the grind. I have parents to ring, suppliers to haggle with. A headmaster's work, as my displaced predecessor might have observed, is never done. My displaced predecessor, by the way, is preparing to go and stay with his wife's sister. She runs a nursing home for the genteel insane, which is in need of an injection of capital. We must hope, must we not, that he is not fleeing from one sinking ship to another?'

He put down his empty glass and got up. But he did not leave, and began tugging at his moustaches with an unusual access of embarrassment.

'Oh—there's one thing I'd better mention, because the police are going to ask about it. It seems two of you had—quite unwittingly—a small part to play in the drama. You, Glenda, I gather, taught him about

Thuggee, did you not? And you, Toby, read them *The Ballad of Reading Gaol* one day when you took over from McWhirter. There were records of both classes in a scrapbook he kept. No blame on you two, of course, but perhaps those two subjects had best be avoided for the remainder of the school year, what?'

And he walked out of the deserted saloon bar.

'Oh my God,' said Glenda.

'Hell's bells,' said Toby.

'What *was* that?' said Dorothea. 'What on earth was he talking about?'

'I think I know,' put in Percy Makepeace. 'Didn't the Thugs—tewibly undesiwable chappies—didn't they—?'

'Make their intended victim feel welcome,' said Glenda, as if remembering her class. 'Made professions of friendship and love for him, did everything to promote his feelings of security, sometimes even aroused affection for the man who was to be his killer.'

'But, I say, he did the same for Onyx,' said Bill, awed by alternative possibilities.

'I taught them all about it,' said Glenda. 'I must admit I enjoyed that class. Went at it with relish. Hilary enjoyed it too, I remember. I'll never tell them about Thugs again. I'll stick to the respectable religions.'

'Ha! Like Mohammedanism, as currently practised in Iran?' suggested Mr McWhirter, repeating his piglet squeal. 'If we suddenly find more and more of our boys missing a hand, we'll know where to pin the responsibility.'

Toby had left his glass untouched since Septimus Coffin's departure, and looked rather sick.

'I'll certainly never teach that poem again,' he said. 'Assuming I ever become a teacher, which I begin to doubt.'

'What was wrong?' asked Dorothea in bewilderment. For Oscar Wilde, not surprisingly, had not figured in

Palgrave's *Golden Treasury*, 1911 edition, prepared for use in the Public Schools. 'What's in it?'

' "Yet each man kills the thing he loves," ' repeated Toby. 'I taught it one day to 4A when McWhirter was sick. "The coward does it with a kiss, The brave man with a sword!" Whenever I read that now I'll see Hilary Frome making up to Malcolm—perhaps making love to Malcolm—and all the time planning to kill him.'

'What was it Hardy said about things that might be bracing to healthy intellects being capable of being used by sick minds?' asked Mr McWhirter. 'The boy intended to kill, remember, and he would have killed whether his teachers had put fancy notions into his head or not. They were just the gilt on the gingerbread. Not that I believe in fancy notions myself, but he could just as well have got ideas from Macbeth killing Lady Macduff's perfectly unbearable little brat, so I'm not going to cast the first stone.'

'This is so *horrible*,' said Dorothea Gilberd. 'One wonders if one can teach *anything*. I just can't believe we're talking about *boys*.'

'One boy,' said Tom Tedder.

'I agree,' said Penny Warlock. 'It's just disgusting. I'm going to see Sep on Monday and tell him that, whatever happens, job or no job, I won't be here after summer.'

'Foolish girl!' said Glenda Grower. 'Do you imagine there are no potential teenage murderers in the state sector? You really must get the message that one simply *does not* give up a job these days. On the contrary, one *claws* one's way into one.'

'She's quite right, Penny,' said Dorothea. 'There simply are no jobs going. I wouldn't get one, with all my experience. And things are going to be better under Sep. Do you know, he's asked me to move with Mother into the head's quarters and take over the supervision of the boarders?'

'I say, how spiffing,' said Corbett Farraday. 'You'd enjoy that.'

'You wouldn't weally, would you?' said Makepeace, awed. 'All those tewible boys. Not a moment's solitude.'

'I'm not all that devoted to solitude,' said Dorothea. 'And of course Toby will be here till summer, to help. But I don't know how things will be . . . There are other considerations . . . There's something —'

'Dorothea and I are thinking of marrying,' said Tom Tedder bluntly.

And after that other considerations, and even Hilary Frome, tended to get forgotten. Penny Warlock, however, did not forget. On Monday after school she went along to Septimus in the headmaster's study and announced her intention to him.

'No, no,' he said, concerned. 'I can't accept that as final. You would be very, very silly.'

'I know, I know, I've heard it all,' said Penny. 'There are no jobs. Cling on to the one you've got —'

'But it's all *true*, dear girl. And if you're thinking that this school won't be here anyway after the summer, then I wouldn't be too sure. I've wooed back most of the parents who wanted to take their treasures away. They're as happy as we are with the outcome. The sensation may even do the school some good. I've had *new* parents inquiring.'

'Oh *no!*' said Penny. 'They couldn't be so awful.'

'Our sort of parent could. It may even give the school a sort of cachet.'

'Well, you don't expect me to find *that* sort of ghoulishness attractive, Sep, do you?' said Penny, her mouth pouting with distaste. 'But anyway it's nothing to do with whether the school will survive or not. It's a matter of what sort of school it is. There's nothing serious to be done here. We're just filling up time for the boys until they're sixteen. It's — I'm sorry, Sep — but it's just an awful school. That's why I want to leave.'

'Of course it's an awful school. My dear girl, you miss the point. Some state schools are good now, some are bad. In ten years' time some of the good ones will be bad, some of the bad ones good. You can't go around insisting on teaching in good schools all your life. Of course we just fill in time, mostly. You're—what?—twenty-three. How much of the trigonometry you learned at school do you remember? Or the chemistry? How much do you think I remember, at seventy-one? The average person has *nothing* left from his education ten years after he leaves school—nothing that he wouldn't have picked up anyway on his own. And that goes for if he went to a good school just as much as if he went to a bad one.'

'Then why do we go on?'

'Because education is prescribed by the state for all children between the ages of five and sixteen. You're looking at it entirely the wrong way round, my dear. You're asking what sort of education this school gives boys. You should be thinking about what kind of people it gives jobs to. Look at us all. Me—a retired, bored schoolmaster, you a young, jobless one. Glenda thrown out of the state system after a totally malicious and fabricated accusation. Teddy a failed artist. Percy a failed everything. We're too old, or we're too young, or we have stains on our characters, or we're flops who need a second chance, or a third or a fourth. Burleigh gives a profession to people like us. Respectable employment. And we fill in the boys' time for them quite as well as most other schools, you'll find. You want to teach classes full of young geniuses with an aptitude for classics. You never will, you know. You may one day have one such pupil, and it's as likely to be at Burleigh as anywhere else. Now, think about it. I want you to be in charge of classics here from now on. I shall be busy playing headmaster, and you'll take over the senior classes from me at once . . .'

You had to give it to him, Septimus Coffin was persuasive. By the time she left Penny had promised to think it over. Septimus walked around his study rubbing his hands with satisfaction. He was getting sharp pleasure out of his Indian summer of authority. Things were coming round remarkably quickly. He had had a most satisfactory talk with Father Michael about a possible future for Percy Makepeace in the Anglican Church. Not orders, because Percy had apparently no more vocation for that than for schoolmastering. But Father Michael had drawn his attention to a position with the Bishop of Sturford, as a personal assistant, a position that could be filled by a layman of a religious turn. And the Bishop of Sturford, apparently, was devoted to chasubles and thuribles and that sort of nonsense. It would suit Percy down to the ground. Then there was the irredeemably Southern League team of Cullbridge, in need of a trainer . . .

Yes, really he felt quite pleased with himself. The clouds were clearing from the face of the sun, and the road ahead stretched clear to the horizon. Under his guidance and leadership Burleigh School seemed set for years to come to fill a modest but dignified position in the private educational system of this country. Hilary Frome, it seemed, would prove to be that figure beloved of Victorian headmasters, the boy who left his school a better place than he had found it.